MARKED BY

Her Bear

THE MONTANA GRIZZLIES 4

ARIEL MARIE

Blurb

One cabin. One storm. One chance to melt the coldest winter.

When her car skidded off a snow-slick mountain road in the middle of Montana, Liana English came to the conclusion that she had the worst luck imaginable. Stranded in a blizzard, injured, with no cell signal, her trip to visit a friend has turned into a nightmare.

Until a towering, gorgeous stranger lifted her out of the storm and into the heat of her cabin fire.

Eddie Fane wanted one week alone—no clan politics, no responsibilities, no expectations. But when her bear heard a crash off in the distance, her instincts roared to life.

Protective. Possessive. Hungry.

Snowed in and forced to share close quarters, sparks ignite between Eddie's desperate need to care for Liana and Liana's stubborn refusal to be helpless. But danger lurked in the woods, and something feral caught Liana's scent…

When Liana disappeared into the storm, Eddie's bear rose—and this time, she won't hold back.

Because once a bear shifter marks her mate…

She'll fight the world to keep her.

If you love steamy, small town sapphic paranormal romance with a possessive bear shifter, then you will enjoy Marked by Her Bear. This story was intended for mature readers only.

Chapter One

Her hands tightened on the steering wheel.
Liana English's rental car slowly made its way
along the two-lane highway. Every mile or so, a
gust of wind pushed the vehicle, rocking it
enough to make her palms sweat. Snowflakes
whirled past the windshield, thick and fast, blur-
ring the world before her.

I shouldn't be out here.

The weatherman had said something about a
winter front blowing in, nothing serious. Just a
typical Montana snow.

What the hell was that supposed to mean?

The farther she drove toward her destination,
the lower the visibility grew, and her gut twisted
in a larger knot. Her phone vibrated in the cup

holder. The display showed it was her younger sister, Jorrie.

She hit the button to the handsfree to connect the call.

"Hello, my favorite sister," Liana answered. She smiled and gripped the wheel harder. "Checking up on me?"

"I'm your only sister," Jorrie replied dryly. "And, why yes, I am. How are the roads?"

"They are just fine. It's bright and sunny. Clear roads, and I even just rolled the window up to answer your call." Liana held back her laugh.

"Liar. It's the middle of winter in Montana. I doubt the people up there have seen the sun in weeks." Jorrie snorted. Her tone alluded that she was in her bossy little sibling mood. "The weatherman is screaming about a nasty storm headed your way. They're saying whiteout conditions. Maybe you should find somewhere to stop."

"There is nowhere to stop except for Lurton, and I think I'm about an hour away. Well, at least if I was going faster than twenty-five miles an hour." Liana groaned. She held the steering wheel steady. Maybe she should have gotten a hotel at the airport and waited this out. But she'd figured she would have made it to Lurton by this time. "All I can see is trees, snow, more trees, snow, and you know what else I see? Snow!"

"Can you turn around?" Jorrie asked.

"No, it's too late. Plus I promised Terri I'd help her with the baby for a week. She hasn't slept in like…I don't know. A month?"

"Where's her husband? He should be helping," Jorrie snapped. Oh, yeah. The little sister was not only in bossy mode but protector mode. "She shouldn't be doing everything."

"Henry is a sweetheart. He's been working double and triple time to make sure they can pay their bills while she's on maternity leave. Believe it, he's doing what he can, because someone still has to keep the lights on," Liana said.

"Well, it certainly was nice of you to volunteer to help her, but maybe you should have waited until next week."

"I didn't know a month ago when I put in the time-off request that Montana was going to get buried in a thousand feet of snow." It was Liana's turn to snort. She sat up taller as she took in the winds picking up and her surroundings turning to whiteout conditions.

"If it gets too bad, just pull over," Jorrie pleaded.

"It's Montana. People do this all the time."

"Yeah, people who *live* in Montana. You're a city girl from Denver who thinks hiking means walking to the coffee shop down the street from your apartment."

"That was one time." Liana rolled her eyes.

"You took an Uber back home!"

"I had on four-inch heels!" Liana gasped. How dare she judge her.

"Exactly! Who wears heels to run out and get coffee?" Jorrie's giggles filled the car.

Liana couldn't help the grin that spread on her face. Jorrie had forgotten to mention the night before they had gone out together and had plenty of wine, which left Liana with a crazy hangover. She'd run to the coffee shop to get caffeine to help with said headache, but Jorrie always left that part of the story out.

Despite the silly back and forth between them, the tension in the car rose. She squinted at the swirling white ahead. Every road sign looked iced over. Every tree bent heavy beneath the amount of snow burdening them. Her heater blasted, but the air inside the car still felt chilled.

"I'm going to be fine," Liana announced for Jorrie, but really for herself. "I'll continue to go slow and steady. I have plenty of gas and I should be there in about an hour. Two if I keep going the speed I'm going."

"Promise me you will call me as soon as you get to Terri's."

"I promise. Love you, big head," Liana whispered.

"I love you, too—"

The line went dead. Liana frowned at her phone. There were no bars. That wasn't a good sign. She was sure it was temporary. The car suddenly felt too quiet.

And it was getting too cold.

She reached for the button to crank the heat up to the highest setting. The snow worsened. It fell in thick sheets, blown sideways by the wind. She slowed down to about twenty miles an hour. Her heart thundered.

"I'm going to be fine," she whispered.

The road curved, lined with thick trees hulking like giants, observing her making the trek. Her headlights did nothing for her. She sucked in a breath and screamed.

Something darted into the road.

A flash of gray.

Liana reacted before her brain actually

caught up. She jerked the wheel to avoid what-ever it was.

Big mistake.

The tires skidded, her traction gone. The world upended. Her stomach dropped as she lost control of the vehicle.

Slam!

The passenger side hit the high snowbank so hard her teeth clicked. Her head smacked the steering wheel, pain rippling through her temple. She tasted copper.

Her car lurched, tilted, then sank deeper into the ditch. The engine sputtered for a moment before dying.

"No!" She tried to start the car again, but nothing. She slammed her hand on the steering wheel. "You have got to be kidding me!"

Cold crept into the car immediately. Panic set it. She tried again to get the engine to start, but it wouldn't turn over. Her ankle throbbed, there was a pounding ache in her head, and something slowly trailed down the side of her face. She tried to move her left leg, but a hot stabbing pain lanced up it. She gritted her teeth to keep from crying out.

"Okay." Her breath puffed white in front of

her. She tried to think. "We've watched enough wilderness survival shows to make it through this."

She rifled through her memories of all of her beloved shows for any tips that could help her.

Build a fire? How? Supplies? She had a blanket, a bottle of water, and a leftover sandwich she had bought at the airport. Well, at least she wouldn't starve or die from dehydration tonight.

Stay in the car? Maybe, but how long would she last until she froze to death? She couldn't even turn the engine on to get some warmth from the heater, but even then, that wasn't a good idea if the exhaust was blocked by the snow.

She reached up and touched her temple. She hissed when her fingers found the cut where the blood was trickling from. Just perfect. She pulled her winter hat farther down on her head in hopes that it would help stop the flow of blood.

"Don't panic," she whispered. It helped to hear her own voice, but panic was taking a hold of her. Minutes passed. Or maybe an hour. Time blurred. The cold made her eyelids heavy and her body tremble. Numbness crawled up her fingers. Her limbs became stiff. It didn't make any sense how cold it was outside. The tremors that racked her body were the only thing keeping her semiconscious.

There was no way she should die this way. She had imagined growing old and passing away in her nineties with her family and loved ones surrounding her.

Not stuck in a ditch in the dead of winter in Montana at the young age of thirty-eight.

A crunch outside the vehicle snapped her awake. Her breaths came fast. The snow shifted slightly. Heavy footsteps grew closer.

Her heart stuttered.

Was it a wolf? A bear? The gray blur that flew out into the road flashed in her mind. She tried to peer out the window, but it was no use thanks to the fogged-up glass and the swirling curtain of snow.

The footsteps stopped outside her car.

A silhouette moved through the thick blizzard, tall and broad-shouldered. Light reflected off dark clothing.

Someone was going to rescue her.

Liana remained still and waited to see who it was. The figure tapped on her window, and she almost jumped out of her skin.

A woman's muffled voice could be heard. "Hey! Are you okay in there?"

Liana fumbled with the door, trying to get it to open. She finally got it to open a half an inch. The howling of the wind increased.

"Yes, I'm here," Liana shouted.

It was then Liana's gaze landed on her rescuer. She was tall with a strong jawline, dark hair that was plastered along her head. Snow clung to her thick eyelashes. Her eyes, amber and intense, flicked to the wound on Liana's head.

"You're injured." Her voice was low, husky, as if she'd been yelling for hours. "Can you walk?"

"I'm not sure. My ankle is killing me. I think it twisted somehow when I hit the bank," Liana said. She winced as she tried to turn to face her.

Liana's rescuer opened the door wider and peered in the car. Her penetrating gaze swept over Liana before narrowing on her. She sniffed once before her nostrils flared.

The woman was a shifter.

There was no question about it.

"My name is Eddie," the woman said. She shouldered the door open and stood near the opening. The gesture blocked the wind and air from blowing directly on Liana.

"I'm Liana," she replied. Liana's gaze swept over her, and she immediately sensed she would be safe with Eddie.

"My cabin is about a quarter mile north from here. You're lucky I head your crash. The woods are too dangerous for a human to sit out here alone," Eddie announced.

Yes, definitely a shifter.

"Something flew across the road. I was trying to avoid hitting it, and that's how I'm in the damn ditch," Liana said. The tremors in her body were overwhelming. Her teeth chattered. She had a winter coat on, but with the current temperatures, she might as well have had on a light jacket.

"It was probably a rogue wolf. They have been causing a lot of trouble up in these parts. Wintertime makes them desperate." Eddie didn't look too happy about the wolves.

Liana attempted to control her body, but the cold was seeping into her bones.

"We need to move. Now." Eddie extended a gloved hand to Liana. She reached inside the car to help her.

Liana tried to shift her weight but cried out at a sharp pain just when she applied her weight to her foot. Liana fell back inside the car. Eddie's reaction was instant. She crouched and slid her arm under Liana's knees and back with surprising gentleness.

"Wait. I can do it," Liana protested. She tried to push her away, but that was like trying to move a brick wall.

"You can't," Eddie said flatly. Her amber eyes practically glowed as she watched Liana. "Your ankle may be injured more than you think. Walking on this terrain will make it worse."

"But—"

"It's freezing. We don't have time. After the storm blows over, I'll come back for your things."

Someone sure is bossy.

Before Liana could attempt to argue again, Eddie lifted her. Heat radiated from the woman in waves. Liana automatically leaned into her, welcoming the warmth. Her scent held faint woodsmoke, pine, and something wild. Liana's cheeks grew hot; she realized she had rested her face into the crook of Eddie's neck while she breathed in her scent.

How embarrassing.

Eddie probably thinks you're a creep.

Eddie slammed the door shut and stepped away from the car. Snow swallowed them as it whipped sideways. It stung Liana's exposed skin. The wind howled so loudly. It was like nothing she had ever heard.

Part scream. Part warning.

She tucked her face against Eddie's shoulder.

"Are you sure you can carry me?" Liana asked. She winced; the throbbing in her ankle worsened.

"You're light." Eddie snorted. "And I'm not a puny little human."

Liana was familiar with shifters. By the size and strength of Eddie, Liana concluded that she must be a bear shifter. Terri, her friend, was a bear shifter, as was her mate.

Still, Liana was impressed by the way Eddie trudged through the knee-deep snow carrying her as if she weighed nothing.

"Keep your head down and hold on," Eddie shouted over the wind.

Liana did as she was told. She tightened her grip on Eddie's jacket. Eddie's muscle movement flexed with each step, and her breath was steady while her heartbeat appeared to remain calm.

Liana felt the soft pulse from the side of Eddie's neck. She nuzzled her face closer and inhaled again. There was something about the scent of her that made her have thoughts she shouldn't be having at a time like this.

Inside Eddie's chest, something rumbled faintly. Something primal, deep with a low vibration. Liana's pulse spiked.

Was that a growl? Or a purr?

"You're making a noise?" Liana whispered. The wind had settled down for a moment.

With her shifter hearing, Eddie heard her. "Ignore it."

The sound would be hard to ignore when it had sent heat spiraling down to Liana's core.

By the time a cabin emerged through the snow, Liana's fingers were numb and pain radiated up her leg. Smoke curled from the chimney, while a warm light glowed through the frosted windows. It was a welcoming sight to behold.

Eddie walked up the few steps of the porch. She stomped her feet to knock some of the thick snow off her legs and boots. She nudged open the door and carried Liana inside. Warmth flowed over Liana, and a sigh escape her.

"Thank goodness," she murmured. The

cabin was rustic with log walls, thick rugs, and a stone fireplace with a crackling fire. It was cozy and safe.

Much better than trying to stay in the car.

Eddie set her gently down on the couch near the fire. She shrugged off her coat, snow dropping to the floor. She moved liked a predator in human skin around the room. She first went over to the fire and stoked it, the flames growing. More heat poured across the room. Liana still trembled, but with the warmth surrounding her, it was lessening.

"Let me see your ankle." Eddie stalked back to her. That amber-eyed gaze of hers dropped down to Liana's foot.

"Okay." Liana first unzipped her coat and wiggled out of it. She winced from the pain that rippled up from her leg as she slid her coat off. She placed it on the back of the couch.

Eddie bent down before her and untied her bootlaces. She held on to Liana's leg while taking her left boot off.

"Ow!"

Eddie frowned, examining Liana's ankle and leg.

"It's just sprained. Not broken but swollen. I

have a first-aid kit. I'll wrap it. You will need to stay off it, keep it elevated and ice it." Eddie stood upright and disappeared into another room.

While she was gone, Liana struggled but successfully removed her other boot. Thankfully, that ankle was fine.

Eddie returned with supplies and a warm blanket. She wrapped Liana up who didn't argue one bit. It was heavenly and smelled faintly of Eddie. She left the room, leaving Liana alone again. She glanced around and took in the simple decor. There was no television, a few books scattered along the coffee table, and some decorations to give the cabin a homey vibe. It would appear that Eddie was alone here. She wondered if Eddie stayed here all year round or was this a getaway home. It appeared to be remote and out of the way from civilization.

Eddie returned a few minutes later with a mug. She handed it to Liana.

"Drink," she ordered.

"What is it?" Liana sniffed it. She eyed the bossy female. She hadn't asked her if she wanted anything, just went and made something. Liana was able to pick up a spicy aroma along with a sweetness to it.

"Honey tea with ginger." Eddie kneeled on the floor before her and began going through her supplies. "It will warm you up faster and help with the shock."

Shock. Well, that would explain the shaking. She sipped it slowly at first. The taste wasn't bad. It wouldn't be something she'd order, but she'd definitely drink it if Eddie thought it would help. Heat bloomed across her chest. Eddie moved closer to her and cleaned the cut on her temple with a gentleness that didn't seem appropriate for someone her size.

"You're lucky," Eddie murmured. "Another hour out there and you'd be hypothermic. Maybe would have lost consciousness."

"Thank you." Liana meant it from the bottom of her heart.

Eddie was right. The odds would have been against her had she stayed out in the car. Eddie's eyes lifted to hers. For a heartbeat, neither of them looked away. Electricity filled the air. Liana's breath caught.

Eddie stood abruptly and took a step back.

She rubbed her hands on her jean-covered thighs.

"We need to get you out of those pants so I can wrap your ankle properly. Don't move." The woman disappeared back into the other room. She sure did give orders without a thought. She must be used to telling people what to do.

Was it the same in the bedroom with her lovers? Heat crept across Liana's cheeks at the thought. She leaned back against the couch, no longer trembling from the cold.

A shiver rippled through her, but this time, it was because of the way Eddie had looked at her.

Like she'd seen something.

Someone she wanted.

Liana raised the mug and took another sip of the tea. What was she going to do? The shifter had elicited a reaction from her that she'd never experienced before.

And from the howling of the wind outside, they may be stuck here together.

For a while.

Chapter Two

The moment Eddie stepped into her bedroom, she pressed a hand to her chest. Her bear paced inside her, right beneath the skin, restless and growling softly.

Mate.

The word was whispered loudly inside her head.

"Not now," Eddie hissed. She went over to her closet and pushed the door open so she could assess what she had that Liana may be able to wear.

Liana was fragile, injured, and held the scent of fear on her. Her cheeks were flushed from the cold. Her ankle was swollen and had needed attention.

But all Eddie's bear wanted to do was nuzzle her, wrap her arms around the woman, and mark her.

Ridiculous.

She grabbed a pair of thick fleece pants, a fitted thermal shirt, and soft wool socks. She muttered a curse. Was Liana going to need help taking her jeans off? They were soaked from the amount of snow that had fallen on them while they had made the walk from her car to the cabin. Eddie shuddered at the thought of seeing Liana's brown thighs. Her dark-brown eyes, smooth brown skin, and plump, kissable lips had immediately caught Eddie's attention. Then her scent hit her, which had sent her bear crazy.

Eddie held the clothing to her chest. She closed her eyes and blew out a deep breath. She had taken this time away from her beloved clan because she needed a break.

One week of peace and quietness.

No commitments. No meetings. No demands.

Just her and her bear spending some time in the wilderness.

Then fate had decided to screw up her plans

and toss a beautiful, injured human directly into her arms.

Her bear didn't care about the logic of the situation. She wanted to claim that woman on the couch now.

Mine.

Eddie clenched her jaw. She could still smell Liana's scent all the way in here. It was sweet, and now nervousness was mixed in. The scent of fear was gone. The woman smelled like cinnamon and honey.

Eddie opened her eyes, unsure what to do. This was the first time she hadn't had a plan. She, the alpha of the Brown Claw Clan, who always had the answers for all those who came to her, didn't have a clue on what she should do about the guest in the other room.

Protect her, her bear rumbled.

I know, Eddie muttered. Then there was the ankle situation. She would focus on taking care of Liana and ensuring she healed properly. She could do this. She was an alpha bear who was in charge of her clan. Why was she hiding in her bedroom as if she were a young cub with her first crush?

She straightened to her full height and

headed back into the living room. Liana tilted the cup back and finished the last of the tea she'd made her. Satisfaction filled Eddie.

"You were right. I already feel much warmer," Liana said. There was a slight tremor in her voice. She set the empty mug down on the table next to the couch.

"Good." Eddie made her way across the room and held up the clothes. "These should fit you. There's a bathroom down the hall where you can get changed."

"You have spare clothing?" Liana blinked.

"Um, yeah. Do you think I only have one outfit?" Eddie smirked. She tilted her head to the side and watched embarrassment wash over Liana's face.

"Well, of course you do," Liana sputtered.

She pulled her hat from her head and dropped it on the couch next to her. She pushed her hair back from her face. The wild ringlets were dark with the tips a golden color. Now that she'd removed her hat, it allowed Eddie to see Liana fully. She was breathtakingly beautiful.

"I mean clothing that will fit me?" Liana clarified.

"We can make them work. You are smaller

than me." Eddie's words ended on a hitch. The size difference between the two of them had her bear in protective mode. Humans were much more fragile than shifters. "Let me help you to the bathroom."

Eddie handed the clothing to Liana with the intention of carrying her. Liana took the clothing and shook her head.

"I can do it." Liana scooted to the edge of the couch and tried to stand. She nearly face-planted on the floor. A cry escaped her lips as she fell back to the couch.

Eddie stood before her and rested her hands on her waist.

The woman was too damn stubborn for her own good.

"Your ankle won't support you. I haven't wrapped it yet. I wanted you out of those clothes and in something loose so I can wrap it good."

"I am not helpless."

"No, but you need help," Eddie replied softly.

Liana's shoulders sagged slightly.

Eddie moved toward Liana and gently picked her up. "I'll carry you for now."

She carried Liana down the short hallway to the bathroom where she sat her on the edge of the tub. The bathroom was small with stone tile, frosted windows, and a faint chill in the air. Liana shivered slightly. Eddie gritted her teeth and backed away to the door.

"I think I've got it from here. I…um…need to use the um…" Liana motioned to the toilet.

Eddie jerked her head in acknowledgment.

"I'll be close by if you need me." Eddie stepped out of the room and closed the door. She leaned against the wall and blew out a deep breath. Her animal prowled inside her as they waited. To give Liana a little more privacy, Eddie went back into the living room and tossed another log into the fire. She had plenty stored on the back porch to keep this fire burning for days. She rushed back into the hall to ensure she'd be nearby when Liana was ready.

"Are you out there?" Liana called.

Eddie opened the door and found Liana in front of the sink. She stood on her good leg while holding on to the sink. Her other foot was kept off the floor. Eddie flicked her gaze down Liana's body. The clothing was quite large on her, but she'd folded the pant legs and the sleeves to make them work for her. Liana's curvy frame was not missed underneath the bigger material.

"I'm here." Eddie picked her up and turned to leave.

"Wait. My clothes."

"I'll get them later," Eddie promised. She carried her back into the living room. She noted that Liana's body felt hotter than when she'd originally brought her into the cabin. "You've warmed up."

"I have. Thank you." Liana sighed.

Back in the living room, Eddie sat Liana down on the thick rug in front of the fire. She wanted to ensure that she was warm. It was freezing outside, and she wanted to keep Liana as heated as possible. She hadn't been out in her car long before Eddie had found her. Any longer and Liana would have certainly frozen to death.

Liana stretched out her injured leg for Eddie. She sat close to her and pulled out the supplies she would need form her emergency kit bag.

"You do this often?" Liana asked.

Eddie carefully pushed up the pant leg and bit back a growl. Liana's soft brown calf was perfectly shaped. It would look good wrapped around Eddie's waist.

She froze and had to control her racing heart. Thoughts such as those should not exist when Liana was injured and trusting her to help her. Eddie swallowed hard and braced Liana's foot on her leg so she could start wrapping it.

"Life as a shifter means there are going to be plenty of injuries," she murmured.

"But I thought shifters healed quickly?" Liana asked with wide eyes.

Eddie smirked at the cuteness of her expression. "We do, but it's not instant. What may take a human weeks to a month to heal, may take us a few days." She certainly had bandaged up enough rambunctious bear cubs who'd forgotten they were not invisible. Or even an enforcer or two who'd got hurt in the line of duty. It was the alpha's job to ensure everyone was protected and safe.

"That's amazing," Liana breathed. Her leg jerked as Eddie was in the middle of wrapping her ankle.

"Hold still," Eddie instructed.

"Sorry. Just a little ticklish." Liana looked away and stared at the fireplace.

Eddie continued to work in silence. She wanted to ensure the wrap would secure Liana's ankle to allow her to put some of her weight on it.

"You said that outside was dangerous. What did you mean by that?" Liana asked.

"It is. Something has been prowling in the woods near the roads, and I don't think it was a normal wolf."

"What would make it not normal?" Liana's head snapped back to her.

Those big brown eyes of hers locked in on Eddie, taking her breath away.

"Desperation. Hunger," Eddie said. She finished wrapping the bandage around Liana's ankle. She reached for the wide tape that she was going to use to hold the bandage in place. This would also lend some support. "Besides, if I hadn't found you when I did, you could have passed out from the cold."

"And then…" Liana's eyes were wide as saucers now.

Her bottom lip trembled, and Eddie could have kicked her own ass. The slight scent of fear reached her from Liana. She hadn't meant to scare the woman.

"You probably wouldn't have woken up."

Liana blinked and looked away. Her chest rose and fell fast. The magnitude of her crash must have sunk in for her. Eddie reached out and took her hand in hers.

"But you're safe now."

Liana's gaze came back to her. The fire cracked, illuminating her smooth skin, warm complexion, and dark lashes. Her hair was wild and free with the ringlets shining bright with their gold tips. Eddie couldn't stop staring at Liana. This woman captivated her. They had only been in each other's presence for a short time, and already she knew she wanted her.

Needed her.

Wanted to put her mark on her.

Liana leaned forward slowly. Eddie's nostrils flared as the sweet aroma of her human's arousal greeted her. A deep, rumbling growl escaped her. It was barely audible, but Liana heard it. She froze in place and tilted her head to the side with a small smile on her lips.

"Are you hungry?" Liana asked.

Eddie blinked then let out a short laugh. She wasn't going to admit what she was truly hungry for, so she lied.

"A bit. I don't remember the last time I ate. I was reading when I heard the crash," Eddie said. Well, she didn't lie all the way. The little white lie didn't sit well with her, but Liana wasn't a shifter so she wouldn't be able to detect the non-truth.

The wind chose that moment to howl. The strength of it rattled the cabin windows.

"Please tell me that was the wind and not a wolf or something looking to eat us," Liana muttered.

"It's the wind," Eddie confirmed. She frowned and listened intently to ensure that it was indeed just the wind, but she didn't pick up anything else. She wasn't going to rest until she was certain they were safe and secured.

Eddie pushed up off the floor and headed to where she'd dropped her coat. She snatched it up and threw it on along with her boots.

"Where are you going?" Liana gasped.

"I'm going to check the perimeter to make sure we're good," Eddie stated. She stalked to the front door and went back out into the storm. The door slammed behind her. The icy cold winds slapped her right in the face. She welcomed the pain of the frozen snowflakes across her skin. It gave her something else to concentrate on other than kissing Liana.

She quickly made her way around the cabin. She pulled the hood of her coat over her head while she assessed the property. All was quiet. Anything would be a fool to be out in this weather. She tromped back to the front door, satisfied that it appeared they would be safe for tonight. With the amount of wolf activity in this area, one couldn't be too sure.

This property had been in her family for years. It was a vacation home that her grandfather had constructed when Eddie's father was a small boy. She had spent many summers and a few winters here with her father. She inhaled sharply as she arrived back at the front door. She had to get her animal in control before she went back inside. She rested her hand on the handle and pushed her bear back down.

The damn animal wanted to break free. Now was not the time. They had to go back inside and see to Liana.

At that thought, her bear settled down.

Eddie went back inside. The moment she closed the door behind her, her bear surged forward, slamming against Eddie's control. The scent of Liana's fear wrapped around her. It took every ounce of strength she had to shove her animal back down.

Calm down, Eddie growled.

Her animal responded with a low rumble in her chest.

She stomped all of the snow off her boots and shook the accumulating snow from her coat and her hair. She took it off and hung it up on the hook by the door. She toed off her boots and walked to the living room.

Liana stood holding the iron poker in her hands like a baseball bat. Eddie froze and held her hands up. Liana's arms shook slightly as she held the poker over her shoulder as if she were about to swing it.

"It's just me," Eddie said softly.

"Well, I had to be sure. You spoke as if you expected unwanted company or something." She lowered the weapon and hobbled back over to the hearth where she returned the poker. "Did you find anything out there?"

"No. Everything's fine. For now," Eddie said. She moved over to the fireplace to check on the flames. The heat felt damn good to her compared to what she had braved outside. She held her hands near the heat for a moment.

"What do you mean, for now?"

Eddie hesitated in responding, but she didn't want to lie to Liana when it came to her safety and the predators that may be lurking out in the wilderness.

"Wolves travel in packs. Even the shifter rogue kind, and that's what I think is out there."

"Rogues?"

"Shifters not abiding by the law," Eddie replied. She stood to her full height. She turned to Liana and took the few steps to stand in front of her. She gazed down on the smaller woman and felt the deep instinct to want to protect her from the world itself. "As long as you stay inside or near me, nothing will bother you."

"Oh?" Liana's perfectly sculpted eyebrow rose. She tilted her head while her gaze did a quick sweep of Eddie. She folded her arms in front of her and studied Eddie. "And why is that?"

"Because there are more dangerous things around here than a wolf?"

"And what is that?" A faint smile tugged at Liana's lips.

"Me and my bear."

Chapter Three

"Oh." Liana chuckled. She smiled and shook her head. That explained the bossiness of Eddie. She was used to being the big bad bear. What animal would dare go up against a bear?

When they were in college, Terri had shared stories of how stubborn and bullheaded her kind could be. Terri was the complete opposite. She was the quiet pushover of their friend group. Liana and Terri had stayed the best of friends even after graduating.

Liana began hobbling over to the couch. Eddie appeared at her side and took her hand to help guide her. The wrappings around her ankle did help. The pain was still there, but at least she could walk without the fear of falling directly on her face.

She eased down on the couch and breathed a sigh of relief. The cabin windows shuddered, and a heavy thunk of snow slid off the roof. Liana jumped.

"This seems to be the storm of all storms." Liana sighed. Maybe she should have tried to turn her car around and gone back to the airport to get a hotel room.

But if she had, she wouldn't have met Eddie.

"Hopefully, it should blow over by tomorrow." Eddie walked over to the window and peered out of it. A second later, the lights flickered.

Once.

Twice.

Then everything went dark.

Liana gasped at the shock of being thrown into the darkness. The cabin grew eerily quiet while the wind continued to howl. A heartbeat later, a dull rumble sounded from somewhere outside. The emergency electricity hummed to life. A dim, golden glow appeared from the kitchen and hall.

Just enough to see shapes, but not enough for Liana to feel completely safe.

"The backup generator," Eddie explained. Apparently, she'd been through this before. She walked back to Liana casually. "It will only power the necessary items. Heat, fridge, and some of the lights. Nothing extra."

Liana swallowed hard. The reality of what was happening settled in. She was thankful she had been found. Winters in Montana could be extremely dangerous.

"So mainly candles and the fire?"

"Yeah. The heat the generator provides will basically keep the pipes from freezing, but it won't warm the entire cabin." She walked over to the cedar chest that was behind the couch. "We will need plenty of blankets. The storm's probably going to get worse, and the temperatures will drop even more. We should keep warm near the hearth."

Liana eyed the thick rug and sighed. She had imagined when she'd arrived to Lurton that she would have a nice comfortable mattress to sleep on, but it looked like the floor in a cabin in the middle of nowhere was where she'd be laying her head for now.

Liana glanced at Eddie as she spread the thick quilts on the floor, layering them like she'd done this a hundred times.

She probably has.

Liana got up from the couch. She needed to help and do something. She couldn't just sit here while Eddie did everything. The moment she stood, her ankle throbbed. She winced. Eddie immediately arrived at her side, her hand hovering near Liana's waist.

Liana blinked and stared up into her amber eyes. The firelight played with the hints of gold that were reflecting in her gaze.

"I'm okay," Liana murmured. She inhaled deeply as the pain slightly lessened. The tight wrappings did help.

"You should sit," Eddie said firmly.

"I can help." Liana motioned to the other blankets that were abandoned in Eddie's rush to get to her side.

"Sit." Her voice dropped slightly.

Something inside Liana wanted to obey. Liana's cheeks warmed slightly; she felt herself complying with the command. She lowered herself back down on the couch. Eddie draped a blanket around Liana's shoulders. Her touch was just a whisper, but it sent an electric jolt through Liana.

The storm continued to shriek. Liana's imagination grew wild. She imaged wolves out there howling with the wind. She stared out the window, and a tremor rippled through her. Had that been what she'd almost hit? Would they try to attack them once the storm was over?

"You're safe here. It's okay." Somehow, Eddie must have picked up on her nervousness. Her hands settled on Liana's shoulders.

Even through the blanket, Liana felt the warmth of her hands radiating through its thickness.

"Are you hungry?" Eddie asked.

Liana blinked. She hadn't thought of food since she had arrived at the cabin. She thought of her half-eaten sandwich that had been left in her car. She shook her head. There was no way she could eat right now.

"I'm not really hungry," she said.

"Well, if you change your mind, there's plenty in the kitchen," Eddie said. She returned to her task of creating them a little nest on the floor before the fireplace.

Liana bit her lip and watched Eddie work.

She tried to slow down her racing heart rate. She didn't want to think of sleeping next to Eddie, but she knew for survival they needed to share heat in order to stay warm.

That was one thing she'd learned from all of the survival shows she loved.

"Come." Eddie stood and motioned for her.

Liana stood again, this time slowly. Her ankle throbbed, but it was tolerable in the short walk to the bedding. Eddie helped her settle down and covered her with the thick blankets. She added another log to the fire before she joined Liana. She came to lie next to her, close enough where their shoulders brushed. She brought the blankets over the both of them.

The fire crackled while the storm continued on.

Here in the dim light and circle of warmth, Liana relaxed. She did feel safe. She glanced over at Eddie who was gazing into the flames. She sighed and rolled over onto her side to face the hearth. She watched the light flicker. The wood splintered and broke into two, the fire consuming it.

"Thank you," Liana murmured.

"For what?"

"For saving me," Liana whispered.

"There's no need to thank me," Eddie said after a pause. "Try to sleep. I'll keep the fire fed."

"But what about you? You're going to need to rest, too." Liana glanced over her shoulder at the bear shifter.

Eddie met her gaze with her lips curled up in the corner. "I'll be fine. Sleep."

Liana wanted to argue, but the warmth of the blankets and the scent of the woodsmoke settled in around her. Fatigue made itself at home inside her, and she couldn't fight it. Liana relaxed and allowed sleep to claim her.

Liana sighed and inhaled deeply. She frowned for a moment, unsure where the hell she was. She was cozy, warm, and a large body that radiated a ton of heat was pressed against her. She inhaled again, and this time she took in a scent that wasn't her own.

She definitely wasn't at home.

There'd be no one sharing a bed with her.

Then it all came back to her. The accident. Trapped in her car. The mountains of snow.

Eddie.

Liana opened her eyes and found herself in the circle of Eddie's arms with her head resting on Eddie's shoulder. She stiffened, unsure when she'd made her way into Eddie's warm embrace. Not that she was complaining. It did feel good, but she wasn't even sure this was appropriate.

Did Eddie have someone? Was she mated? In a relationship?

Body heat will help with survival. Those words echoed in her head. Maybe she could play this off when Eddie woke up. Currently, the bear shifter was resting with her eyes closed, which gave Liana a chance to really study her.

She was gorgeous with her long dark eyelashes, and her thick hair was pulled back from her face in a ponytail. Liana would love to see what it would look like spread along her silk pillows. Those amber eyes of hers made Liana's core clench. Thankfully, she couldn't see them since Eddie was asleep.

Liana's breath caught in her throat at the thought of Eddie's physical form. She was pressed close to her and could feel every curve, every firm muscle the woman possessed. It was unfair how shifters didn't even have to try to be fit. Liana had to work out constantly to keep her form, and if she ate like a bear shifter, she'd been round like a clock.

Liana snuggled closer to her. She wasn't going to feel any type of shame. It was the first time in a long while that she'd woken up in the arms of a beautiful woman. She was going to take full advantage of this. Even if it was for one night. Liana thought back to her last relationship, and it had been a few years. She had been celibate because every girl in her past had been either jealous or deranged in the head.

She'd never been involved with a shifter before.

And why would you be now? Liana sighed. She was sure Eddie wasn't interested in someone like her. Someone who'd almost died because of her carelessness. She should have paid attention to the weather reports. Stayed at a hotel until the storm blew over then traveled to Lurton.

Lesson has been learned.

Eddie shifted slightly, her arm sliding down Liana's back. Liana bit back a moan when her hand came to rest on the small curve of her back. A few inches farther and Eddie's hand would be on her ass. Eddie breathed deeply, and her breasts pressed against Liana's.

"Are you warm enough?" Eddie's voice rumbled beneath her ribs.

That sound she'd heard before that resembled a purr vibrated from Eddie's chest. Liana glanced up and was met with the heated amber gaze of her bear shifter.

"Um, yeah. Thank you." Liana licked her lips.

Eddie's gaze dropped to her lips. The heat in her eyes flared even more. Butterflies filled Liana's stomach. She didn't know how long they had slept or how long she had been in Eddie's arms.

"No problem. I noticed you shivering again, so I thought to bring you closer to me," Eddie said.

Ah. She was helping her as she'd slept.

Well, that makes sense.

"You just know how to take care of me, don't you?" Liana joked. She closed her eyes and leaned her forehead down to put her face back in the crook of Eddie's neck. She wasn't going to lie, she didn't want to move from this spot.

"Yeah, I do. If you'd let me," Eddie said.

"What is that supposed to mean?" Liana gasped. Her head flew back so she could see Eddie's face.

The woman stared at her with an expression that Liana couldn't read.

"You are injured. Allow me to help you," Eddie said softly. Her hand came up to gently cup Liana's face.

Liana leaned into the callused palm. This was someone who worked with her hands. Liana immediately fantasized what it would feel like to have those hands running along her bare thighs. A shiver rippled through her.

Eddie's eyebrows rose. "Still cold?"

"No." She was far from cold. If anything, she was starting to overheat being this close to Eddie. She looked away from her. "I just don't want to feel helpless. You have done plenty for me. The least I can do is help out around here to pay you back."

"You don't ever have to pay me back," Eddie snapped. She narrowed her eyes on Liana.

Her expression of anger took Liana's breath away.

Eddie tightened her hold on Liana's face.

"You were trapped, injured, and in danger. Any decent person would have—or at least should have—helped."

"But still. It's just in my nature to—"

"To be stubborn?" Eddie's expression softened. Her thumb softly caressed Liana's face.

The move could be felt all the way down to Liana's core. Her breaths came swiftly as she focused on the swipes of her thumb.

"Determined. Helpful," Liana retorted, her eyes fluttering shut.

This woman was doing things to her that made her body come alive. What was this between them? Was Eddie feeling it, or was this all one-sided because it had been a long time since Liana had felt the touch of another in such an intimate way?

"Hmmm…" Eddie murmured. Her thumb paused its movement.

Liana opened her eyes, and her heart skipped a beat. Eddie lowered her head and paused when their lips were millimeters from each other. Liana parted her lips slightly. Eddie groaned and closed the distance between them.

Her lips were firm yet soft. Liana's opened to welcome Eddie's bold tongue that swept inside her mouth. Liana lifted her arms to wrap them around Eddie's neck. Unable to resist, she tugged Eddie to her. She didn't want the woman to pull away—not yet.

The kiss was heated and possessive. Eddie wasted no time in dominating it. She held on to Liana's head while her tongue plundered. Liana wasn't shy in meeting her in the kiss. She returned it with such a fire that it left both of them breathless when they drew apart. They stared at each other for a moment before Eddie spoke.

"I'm sorry. I shouldn't have—"

"Please don't apologize. I mean, unless you have a mate or something," Liana breathed.

"What? I don't have a mate," Eddie replied.

"Then why are you apologizing?" Liana's fingers played with the small amount of hair that had escaped Eddie's ponytail at the base of her neck.

There was conflict in Eddie's amber gaze. She glanced down at Liana and blew out a deep breath. "Because I don't want you thinking I am taking advantage of you."

Chapter Four

Eddie stood by the window and took in all of the snow that pressed against the window in thick layers, but the storm had passed. At least for now. Her gaze drifted to Liana who was still curled up on the blankets she had arranged for them last night. Her skin glowed from the light of the hearth.

She'd kissed her. Eddie inhaled, still remembering how it had felt to experience Liana's lips against hers. It had been tender at first then passionate. Eddie hadn't been able to resist taking Liana's plump lips. The desire to taste them had weighed heavy on her the moment Liana had licked them. She would have to restrain herself. Her bear, not understanding, prowled in her chest.

She had felt guilty the second they had broken away.

I don't want you thinking I am taking advantage of you.

She shouldn't have touched her, and she certainly shouldn't have kissed her. She hadn't lied when she'd said that Liana had been shivering. She'd noticed Liana shaking, so she'd brought her into the circle of her arms. Shifters' body temperatures ran hotter than humans. The moment she'd had Liana in a hug, the female settled down. It had been tortuous for Eddie, but she'd managed.

Her bear was growing restless and impatient. She wanted to claim Liana immediately, but now wasn't the time. Eddie had to fight her bear to keep her in check. Liana was injured. She wouldn't be ready for what it would mean to be claimed.

Eddie wasn't sure if Liana understood the shifter ways.

A groan came from the blankets. Eddie blinked and focused again. It wasn't like her to not be in tune with her surroundings. Liana was standing; the blankets had fallen to the floor in a heap.

"What are you doing?" Eddie said.

Her first instinct was to rush over to her. Liana would complain. Her little human was determined and stubborn.

"Nature is calling," Liana admitted sheepishly.

"Let me help you." Eddie walked across the room toward her.

Liana shook her head. "Eventually, I need to walk short distances. The bathroom isn't that far. I can make it." She turned and limped toward the hall. She paused and rested a hand on the wall and glanced at Eddie over her shoulder. "Any chance you have an extra toothbrush?"

"Yeah. Look in the cabinet in the bathroom. It's stocked with everything you would need." Eddie was thankful her family kept the cabin supplied with goods. Once she left, it would be her turn to ensure it was ready for the next family member who would want to utilize the cabin.

Liana gave a nod and disappeared down the hall. Eddie used her shifter hearing and listened. Her muscles tensed as she waited to hear if

Liana ran into trouble, but the only sound that greeted her was the bathroom door slowly closing.

She ran a hand over her face. Liana would be fine. Her bear growled in her chest.

Mate.

Eddie rolled her eyes and made her way into the kitchen. Her bear was not going to rest until Eddie did something about Liana. She went over to the sink and washed her hands before she prepared their meal. Liana would need nourishment in order to heal properly. She would make them a simple breakfast. The power was still out, but thanks to their gas stove, she could still cook on the stovetop. She gathered the supplies to make them some oatmeal. That would be a good hearty meal for her mate.

Eddie froze. She had to stop thinking of Liana as hers, or her mate. Humans didn't feel what shifters did. There was a chance that Liana would reject her and her bear.

But that kiss led Eddie to believe Liana felt something for her.

A hiss of pain sounded from the door. Eddie turned and found Liana standing in the doorway of the kitchen. She was there next to her in a heartbeat. Liana had braided her hair down into two plaits. Her wild hair was now tamed. Eddie didn't know which look she preferred.

"Have a seat," Eddie murmured. She eyed Liana's leg and wondered if she needed to redo the wrap. It seemed as if it were still holding. She'd take it down in a little and reassess Liana's ankle to make sure everything was okay.

"I can't. I need to help with something," Liana protested.

"Your ankle is obviously telling you that you're doing too much." Eddie guided Liana over to the small island and helped her up on to a chair. She bit back a smile at the expression of determination on Liana's face. "I am going to make a simple breakfast. Oatmeal and toast. I won't need any help with that."

"Are you sure you won't need me to do anything?"

The woman refused to back down from carrying her own weight. Eddie couldn't help but respect it. She shook her head and rested her hands on Liana's knees. Her bear growled in her chest, a deep vibration that tensed her muscles.

Mine.

Eddie pressed the thought down and forced

herself to focus on what she was saying. Liana's eyes had grown wide as saucers.

"You're making that sound again. Is that…is that your bear?" Liana asked. Her gaze dropped down to the center of Eddie's chest as if checking to see if she could see Eddie's beast.

Her bear was impatiently waiting to meet her. It would be a while before Eddie would allow her bear to come out and meet Liana. Not that she'd hurt Liana. It was that she needed to make sure Liana was comfortable with her being a bear.

Hell, she had to make sure Liana was comfortable with Eddie pursuing her.

"It is, but ignore her. She's grouchy in the morning," Eddie lied. She hated speaking untruths, but she didn't want to let on to Liana what was really going on with her animal. There would be plenty of time later for that.

"If you say so," Liana murmured.

Eddie moved around the kitchen, gathering what she needed. She felt Liana's eyes watching her. She could tell the woman was curious about her. There was a slight hint of attraction in the air. Eddie tried to ignore it as she worked. Her bear nipped at her, wanting her to address it. While waiting for the water to boil in the pot, she made both of them a cup of hot tea. With the low wind-chill outside, they would need to stay warm inside. She had built the fire back up when she awoke to ensure the living space was nice and toasty.

"Here you go." Eddie handed Liana her mug.

Their fingers brushed each other's. The contact was brief, but enough. Heat surged through Eddie. She flexed her fingers and resisted the urge to touch Liana or worse—kiss her again.

Right now, she had more things she needed to focus on than kissing this beautiful woman.

"This tea is good. You are going to have to share your recipe. I'm usually a coffee drinker, but this right here, I could drink every day," Liana admitted. She stared down into her cup.

"It's a simple recipe. My grandmother actually taught me when I was younger. She used to grow her own leaves to make tea," Eddie said. She went back to the stove and continued making their breakfast. She gave the oatmeal a good stir to ensure it wasn't burning and turned down the flame. She glanced over at Liana and wondered how she liked her oats.

"Well, I want to know one thing about bears," Liana said. She smiled and set her mug down on the counter.

"And what is that?" Eddie faced Liana and leaned back against the counter. She folded her arms in front of her so she could pay attention to what her mate—Liana—wanted to know. She would be open about her kind. She wanted Liana to know everything there was about her and the clan.

"Is it true that bears love honey?" Liana giggled.

Eddie relaxed and gave a hearty chuckle. Liana's giggles turned into a fully fledge laughing fit with tears running down her face and all. She made such a cute picture when she smiled. It was good to see that she was in light spirits. After almost dying yesterday, it was nice for her to find humor.

"Well, I can't speak for all bears, but this one right here definitely has a sweet tooth," Eddie admitted.

Liana fell into another fit of laughter. She wiped her face and shook her head. "I'm sorry, but I always ask. My friend, who I was going to visit, she's a bear shifter, and it was one of the first questions I asked her when we met in college." She sniffed. Her smile and laughter were infectious.

"So that's why you were out in this storm? To visit a friend. Is she deathly ill or something?" Eddie asked. It had to be the only reason a person would attempt to travel in this weather.

"Um, no. I thought I could make it to Lurton before the storm hit, but boy did I misjudge." Liana's smile disappeared.

So she was going to Lurton. Interesting.

"Who is your friend?" Eddie asked casually. As the alpha of the clan, she knew almost everyone by name. Their clan wasn't the largest one around, but she tried to get to know as many bears as she could.

"Terri Collins. She recently had a baby, and I was going to stay with her for the next week. Henry has been working so much that I told her I wouldn't mind coming to help her out." Liana lifted her mug and took another sip of her drink.

"Ah, yes. Terri. I know her and Henry," Eddie said. The Collinses were longstanding members of the Brown Claw clan. She was familiar with him and his parents. "Junior is a cute little baby."

"I know. She's sent me so many pictures. He has the fattest cheeks. That's why I was trying my best to get to them. His aunt Liana needs a good hug and cuddles." Liana sighed.

Eddie bit back a groan at the thought of cuddling with Liana again. Last night had been torture. Fantasies of what they could have done kept creeping into her mind. It had made it hard for Eddie to fall asleep, and when she finally had, Liana had been right there in her dreams.

"Well, I certainly see why you braved the weather. I'll make sure you make it to Lurton safely," Eddie said. She turned around and went back to the oatmeal. It had thickened up perfectly and was ready. She used a skillet to toast their bread. "Brown sugar, cinnamon, and butter for your oatmeal?"

"How'd you know?" Liana gasped.

Eddie smiled and shrugged while she flipped the bread over. "That's how I take mine." She chuckled. She took the toast off the skillet and placed it on a dish and turned off the gas.

"Here, I can get the bowls. Where are they?"

Eddie turned back and found Liana already

carefully making her way to the cabinets. She began opening them one by one until she found them. Eddie folded her arms in front of her and stared at her.

Liana turned back around with two bowls in her arms. "What?"

"You are supposed to be—never mind." Eddie shook her head. This woman just refused to allow her to take care of her. She moved over to her and took the bowls from her. "You are impossible."

There was no harshness to her words. They shared a look before Liana glanced away. Liana had balanced herself on her good leg. Eddie's free hand went out and rested on her waist to hold her steady.

"I know. You'll get used to it," Liana said softly. Her eyes flicked back to Eddie's.

Eddie set the two bowls down so she could lift and carry Liana back to her chair, but something in Liana's eyes gave her pause. The tension between them sizzled. Liana leaned forward and pressed her lips to Eddie's.

Eddie's heart slammed in her chest. This kiss was heated, desperate even, and charged with an earth-shattering desire. Liana's hands slipped upward to her hair and pulled the tie free. They entwined themselves in Eddie's dark tresses. Eddie held Liana to her while she took over the kiss. It was in her nature to lead, and with Liana, she would always be the one to take control. Her bear paced beneath her skin as the kiss deepened. Eddie spun them around so Liana was trapped between the counter and her.

Her hands traveled down the length of Liana until they rested on her ample ass. It was soft and plump. Even Eddie's larger hands couldn't hold all it in her palm. She loved a woman who had curves and a nice ass. The two of them fit perfectly together.

Eddie pulled back just enough, her breaths coming hard. The scent of Liana's arousal permeated the air. As much as she wanted to continue this, they couldn't.

Liana is injured. Not yet.

Liana's lips were swollen, and it took everything Eddie had to not plunder them again. They were sweet and addicting. She inhaled sharply and combed her fingers through her hair.

"I'm supposed to be feeding you," Eddie said. She cleared her throat after hearing the huskiness that had taken over. She kept her hand on Liana's waist and helped guide her back to the chair.

"I just really wanted to kiss you again," Liana murmured.

Eddie paused next to Liana. Her hands slid down from her waist and rested on her knees.

"Well, I'm glad you did. Now let me feed you." Unable to resist, she placed a gentle, chaste kiss on Liana's lips. She backed away before she did something she would regret later. She spun around and snagged the bowls from where she'd left them. She quickly fixed their oatmeal and toast. She set everything out on the island. She grabbed everything they would need before she took the seat next to Liana.

They ate their meal in a comfortable silence that was lined with sexual tension. Eddie's bear continued to pace back and forth, occasionally butting her head against Eddie's chest. Eddie glanced over at Liana and took in her few strands of hair that had sprung from her braids. It rested along her cheek, ignored while Liana ate.

"This is so good," Liana murmured. She took another bite of her toast that she had slathered with strawberry jam. A small moan escaped her as she continued to eat.

Mine. All mine.

Her bear slowly calmed down. They were attending to their mate, and she was loving the food that Eddie had prepared. Her bear settled down and continued to watch Liana. For now, Eddie's beast grew silent.

Eddie turned back to her bowl and dove right in. She had a lot to do today now that the storm had blown over, and she would need her energy.

Eddie assisted Liana back toward the couch with one arm braced around her waist to keep her balanced. The stubborn woman tried to hide the slight limp in her step while her jaw was tight with determination. Eddie felt every wobble she tried to hide. Her bear growled low, urging her to lift and carry Liana. She ignored it. Liana was determined to walk.

"Easy," Eddie murmured. She guided her

down on to the sofa. "You're putting too much weight on that ankle."

"I'm trying not to," Liana muttered. She winced and settled onto the cushion.

Eddie crouched in front of her. She unwound the makeshift brace she'd tied last night. The moment the bandage loosened, the faint swelling around the joint was revealed. It wasn't bad, considering Liana had been in a car accident, but enough to worry her.

"You're lucky it's just sprained," Eddie said. She gently prodded the swollen area. "We could have been dealing with a fracture."

Eddie continued assessing Liana's ankle. She tried to ignore how cute Liana's toes looked with their pink polish, or how small her feet appeared to be. She traced along the outer edge of the ankle to check for tenderness. Had the wrap been too tight? She didn't think so, but she would ensure she did better next time. Liana's breath hitched, barely audible, but Eddie caught everything.

Even the way Liana's heart rate skyrocketed.

"There is some slight bruising, but that will fade with time. Other than that, it looks good," Eddie admitted.

"I'm a fast healer," Liana said.

"Oh, you've broken bones and sprained ankles before?" Eddie arched an eyebrow at her and watched Liana. A smile played on her lips when Liana tried to hide a laugh behind a cough.

"No." Liana rolled her eyes and turned away, but not before Eddie caught her smile.

Eddie rewrapped the ankle with steady hands. Once she was satisfied that Liana's ankle was secured and the material wasn't too tight, she twisted Liana's body around so she could rest her feet on the couch. She stood and snagged a pillow and placed it underneath Liana's foot.

"Elevate and rest," Eddie ordered.

"Like, all day?" Liana blinked at her. She scrunched up her face and shook her head. "And do what on the couch? Just sit here and look pretty?"

"There's nothing wrong with that," Eddie murmured. She could stare at Liana all day and never tire of her beauty. She blew out a deep breath; she had work to do outside. She needed to assess the property and see what damage may be awaiting her.

"You're just saying that because—" Liana paused whatever she was about to say.

"Because?"

"Oh, never mind. You're going to chill here with me, right?" Liana asked.

"Actually, I need to go outside for a bit. I need to make sure the storm didn't damage the cabin, check the generator to make sure the lines haven't iced over, and maybe clear some of the snow." Eddie looked at the pile of wood near the hearth and made a mental note to grab some more logs. The main electricity hadn't come back on yet. There was no telling how long that would take. The last time a storm this bad had blown in, it had taken a week before the power had been restored.

"Wait outside? I could go and get some fresh air?" Liana sat forward.

"No." Eddie's voice was firm.

Liana eyes narrowed on her. She folded her arms in front of her chest.

Eddie didn't care if her mate was going to be mad at her. She was going to have to draw the line somewhere. "You're staying inside in the warmth so you can rest."

"Why?"

"Because you are injured," Eddie bristled. "The snow may be too thick. You can slip and fall and re-injure your ankle."

"Let me guess, and it's also dangerous out there?" Liana arched an eyebrow.

"Exactly." Eddie did need to do a perimeter check. If Liana's crash was due to a wolf, she needed to make sure that wolf stayed far away from her property. Her top priorities when it came to Liana were keeping her safe and taking care of her.

"Why can't I just stay close to you?" Liana taunted. She shrugged and continued. "I won't go far, and it will allow me to get some fresh air."

"No."

"I promise, I will be fine."

"Liana." Eddie pinched the bridge of her nose. She inhaled sharply and tried to shove down her irritation. Why didn't her mate see it was best for her to stay inside while she went out and did some work? Eddie wouldn't be able to concentrate fully if she had to worry about Liana.

Liana batted her lashes—slow, deliberate, practiced. Eddie felt the hit in her gut like a punch. The woman certainly knew what she was doing.

Never had someone defied her as much as this woman had in such a short time. Eddie was an alpha, and many heeded her words without complaints or pushback.

This woman knew how to press every button.

"It's a little stuffy in here," Liana whispered. "And I swear I won't go far. My boots are right by the door, and this wrap is pretty tight. I'd practically have armor around my ankle."

"What if you fall?"

"You'll be right there to catch me. A big strong bear like yourself won't let me get hurt again." She did that thing again with her eyelashes.

The compliment, intentional or not, sent a warmth through Eddie's chest. The bear inside her all but rolled over to show her belly for Liana.

"You are trouble," Eddie murmured.

"I know." Liana gave her a sweet smile. "So…can I?"

Eddie stared at her. Liana's big brown eyes sparkled as she waited for Eddie's answer. Her scent curled into Eddie's senses. It was warm, buttery almond mixed with something sweet like honey. Eddie's bear nudged her.

Eddie sighed. She was doomed.

"Fine," she relented. She pointed a stern finger at Liana and gave her a soft menacing glare. "Let me clear some of the snow off the deck where you are to stay. No steps. No wandering around."

"Yes, ma'am." Liana gave her a playful salute. "Just help me put on my boots and coat, and I won't need you for anything else."

Eddie sighed. She had a funny feeling she was going to regret this. How was she a strong alpha bear who ruled an entire clan, but when it came to this woman, she became a cuddly teddy bear?

Chapter Five

The cold air was crisp and sharp. Liana breathed in, shivering slightly. She leaned against the door while she watched Eddie clear the deck off. The woman was making light work of the mountains of snow that had accumulated there. Had Eddie not told her there was a deck out back, she never would have known. The amount of snow that had fallen was incredible.

The snow glittered like crushed diamonds across the mountains off in the distance. The sunlight caught the frost-heavy branches and sparkled brightly. The storm had passed, leaving the world bleached white and so quiet she could hear her own breaths.

"It's so beautiful." Her exhalations fogged the

air in white swirls. To think that just yesterday she'd thought she was going to freeze to death, and now she was admiring the wonder in what Mother Nature had created.

Maybe being stranded wasn't the end of the world.

Her gaze landed on Eddie who quietly shoveled along the edge of the deck, clearing heavy drifts away. Even bundled in a thick jacket, the woman appeared to be the epitome of strength. Her shoulders were solid, her movements efficient and focused. Every time she exhaled, it fogged the air like a dragon in the cold.

But Eddie wasn't a dragon, she was a bear.

Liana wondered what Eddie's beast looked like. Was she a brown bear? A black bear? How tall did she get? Was she ferocious? A cuddly bear? Liana snorted at that thought. It amazed her that a shifter's body could literally change into something else completely. Would Eddie allow her to meet her bear?

"You're enjoying the view." Eddie's voice broke through Liana's thoughts.

She blinked and focused on the woman who had paused what she was doing to stare at her. Liana smiled and took an easy step down on to the deck. She pulled the door closed behind her. She took another careful step. So far, so good.

"I am, and how could I not?" Liana made her way to the railing and paused. She celebrated on the inside that she hadn't slipped and the pain was only slight now. She motioned to the snow-covered grounds. "It looks picture-perfect. Like it should be on a postcard or something."

"It looks like hypothermia waiting to happen," Eddie muttered. She turned and faced the endless amounts of snow that covered the yard. She jammed the shovel into a pile. "Stay up on the deck while I check the generator. I need to make sure she isn't going to choke tonight. I smell another storm brewing."

Liana nodded, then watched Eddie disappear around the side of the cabin.

The fresh winter air felt good. Even though it was cold, she felt a little freedom now that she wasn't secured away inside the cabin. A girl could only be locked up so long. She sighed. If Eddie sensed there was going to be a part two of the storm, that wasn't good. How the heck would she get to town? How would she be able to get her car towed to a shop?

There was so much that she would need to take care of. She didn't want to think about notifying the rental company of the accident. Thankfully, she had good insurance that should cover things.

She wasn't going to think of that now. She was safe and secure, and that was what really mattered. She stood on the top stair and balanced her weight carefully, testing her ankle. The wrap held. It pinched a little, but nothing crazy. This was definitely manageable compared to when she'd had nothing to help secure the joint.

Liana's gaze drifted beyond the tree line. The storm had blown down a chunk of foliage, which opened up a view she hadn't noticed before.

And faintly, she heard water.

A steady trickle through the quietness.

Was that a creek? Or a river? How was it not frozen over in these temperatures?

Her pulse fluttered. A peek wouldn't hurt. A short walk would help her stretch out her aching muscles, and she could test out her ankle more. She couldn't stay laid up all day, every day. That wouldn't be good for her. She may not be a nurse or a physician, but she knew that much.

Eddie must have cleared more of the snow before she had come outside. There was a small path that led to the tree line.

"Just a short walk. I need this fresh air," she murmured. She zipped up her coat all the way and tugged her hat down on her head.

She stepped off the deck.

She paused and glanced around, half expecting Eddie to come charging around the corner to yell at her. When there was no bossy bear coming to bark orders, she continued. Her boots crunched through the light snow on the path. Pine trees towered overhead. A slight breeze created a slight snow flurry from the snow being shaken loose from the limbs. The cold nipped at her nose and cheeks, but something in the air had her pulse racing.

She breathed in the frosty air and smiled.

The farther she walked, the louder the creek sounded.

"There you are." The water came into view. Icy water rippled along the bank of white edges crusted with thin sheets of ice. She crouched carefully and marveled at the beauty of the scene before her. Back home when she couldn't sleep, she played soothing sounds and usually chose creeks or ocean waves. There was something about the sounds of water that helped her relax and sleep.

She reached out and brushed snow from a rock. It was an unusual color of onyx. Was this supposed to be here? She tried to pry it loose with the intention of taking it back to the cabin as a souvenir. She bit her lip and used a little more force and jerked back. The rock came free. She scooped it up and stood to her full height. She held it up toward the sky so she could observe it. The rock was smooth and reminded her of pure marble. It was a beauty, and she figured she could give it a good home back in Denver.

She turned to go back, and her boot slid.

Everything happened too fast, her foot finding a patch of ice under the snow. She tilted backward, her arms flailing like windmills.

"No...no...no—"

Her feet flew out from under her, and the world practically flipped upside down.

Cold water swallowed her.

The creek wasn't deep, but the shock of the cold water was a brutal slap to her. It immediately wrapped around her bones and took her breath away. She gasped and swallowed a heaping amount of the freezing water as she plunged underneath the surface.

Her head popped up. She sputtered and glanced around. The cold was cutting through her as she tried to right her footing.

Pain exploded through her ankle and up her leg. Water surged around her. It was numbing, and her teeth chattered. Her heartbeat slammed against her chest. The current of the water was angry and determined to pull her under again.

"Come on," she groaned. She tried to kick and find traction. Her ankle buckled again. The pain was unbearable. She bit back a sob, panic surging through her. She clawed at the stone and dirt along the bed of the creek. She couldn't grasp hold of anything.

The Discovery Channel tips for surviving the wild were nowhere to be found in her head. The only thing she remembered—stay calm.

That was easier said than done. They weren't currently trying to get dragged down a strong creek in the wintertime in the middle of Montana.

With a groan, she angled her body sideways, finally able to hook her arm over a rock jutting from the mud. Gasping, she managed to drag herself halfway out of the water. Her legs were still submerged while her boots were heavy with creek water.

She froze.

Not from the temperatures, but from a sound.

Something cracked in the woods. Nothing soft. A sharp snap.

Whatever it was tried to be stealthy.

"Eddie?" she called. Her voice trembled slightly. She frantically searched the area, trying to see what was in the woods.

The only response was silence.

Her heart rate raced even faster, her breaths coming in pants. It was watching her. She could feel it. Icy fingertips slipped between her shoulder blades. She twisted around and still didn't see anything. The trees stood motionless. No wind. No birds.

Just a freaky stillness.

Her mind raced. She remembered Eddie warning her that the area was not safe. That wolves could be roaming the area. Rogue wolves, was it? She swallowed hard.

Another crack.

Whatever it was, was moving closer.

The cold was stealing what was left of her strength. Her teeth were clattering out of control.

There!

A figure stood hidden deep in the woods. Tall. Muscular.

And it was not Eddie.

Raw terror filled her, and there was nothing else she could do at the moment but one thing.

"Eddie!"

Eddie knocked another chunk of frozen snow from the generator housing with her gloved hand. The unit hummed steadily beneath the metal casing, but she didn't trust it. Her cousin had assured her that he'd had the generator checked before the first snow when he and his mate had used it.

But had he?

She just hoped it continued working fine with

the pressure dropping and that heavy warning in the air.

Another storm was coming soon.

She crouched to brush more off the intake vents, her breath clouding in the air. The temperature was certainly bottoming out. She was glad she had enough firewood to keep them warm for a while. She stood and paused.

The wind shifted. Her head snapped around. There was an eerie silence in the woods. Everything was too still. The hairs on the back of her neck lifted. She inhaled slowly and tried to place it.

The scent of the water.

Human fear.

Panic.

She turned slowly in the direction of the water. Liana wouldn't have left the safety of the deck. Eddie had warned her that the area was dangerous for a human. She took a step forward and paused. Her ears only picked up one sound.

"Eddie!"

The sound of Liana's scream punched through the trees like a gunshot. Eddie's heart slammed against her chest. She was already sprinting before she could form a conscious thought. Her boots tore through the packed snow, a growl rising in her throat. Her bear surged forward, ready to take over. Eddie's senses sharped as her bear pressed on.

Branches whipped past her. She pounded the earth, and snow exploded. She rounded the corner and found tracks leading to the water.

Dammit! Liana hadn't listened to her. Eddie pushed faster until she came to the clearing. She skidded to a halt and saw her. Liana had hauled herself halfway onto the muddy bank, completely soaked. Her body was racked with tremors. Her hat was no longer on her head, and her wet hair clung to her cheeks.

"Eddie," Liana gasped. "Something was in the woods. It was watching me—"

Liana's voice ended on a sob. The fear that radiated from her sent Eddie's bear into a rage.

"Don't move." Eddie dropped to her knees beside her. Her voice came out much steadier than she expected. Her gaze swept the tree line. No movement, but—

Her nostrils flared. Her bear gave a low warning growl.

Wolf.

A snarl tore through her chest. She couldn't

shift now and go after the animal. She had to attend to Liana who was soaked and freezing.

But her bear understood they needed to see to their mate first. That was their top priority. Hunting down the rogue wolf that had caused fear in Laina would have to wait.

For now.

"How did you fall in?" Eddie asked.

"I wanted to take a short walk to stretch out my muscles. I wanted to see the water. I could hear it. I couldn't believe that it was not frozen. I slipped—" Liana's teeth chattered, which made it hard for her words to come out clear.

Eddie's jaw flexed. Stubborn woman. When was she going to learn to listen to her? She had given her specific orders to stay on the deck but she'd ignored her.

"You're okay. I'm here." Eddie reached for Liana and pulled her completely away from the water. She did a quick sweep of Liana's form and didn't see anything broken, but she was soaked and freezing.

"I know I saw something in the woods. It disappeared when I screamed."

Eddie's stomach dropped. Rogue wolves liked to hunt by scent, stalk the weak, and an injured human who disobeyed orders would be a beacon for any who were nearby.

Eddie didn't need to see what Liana had seen. The wind assisted her. The wolf had been extremely close to Liana.

"We're getting inside. Now." Eddie hooked an arm around Liana's back and lifted her.

Liana winced as her sprained ankle moved. Eddie cradled her against her chest. Liana gasped and gripped Eddie's jacket.

"You don't have to —"

"Shut it, woman," Eddie growled. Now was not the time to argue about being carried.

Eddie spun around and made her way toward the cabin. Heat radiated from her body automatically. Liana leaned into her. It should have felt good to have her woman in her arms, but not under these circumstances.

A dark object in Liana's hand caught Eddie's attention. Upon closer inspection, it looked like a black, smooth, glossy rock.

Was that how Liana had fallen into the creek? Because of a rock?

"Why do you have that?" Eddie muttered.

Liana clamped her fingers around it tighter and pressed it to her chest.

"I found it near the creek. It's beautiful, and I wanted to keep it as a souvenir to take back home."

Eddie's bear bristled at the thought of Liana leaving them. Her jaw clenched tight with the idea of not having Liana around. In their short time together, Eddie already knew she would do what she must to convince Liana to stay.

Her clan had been very adamant that she needed to take a mate. Eddie had focused her entire life on ensuring her clan was for the better. Even before she'd assumed the title, she had been raised and groomed for the role of alpha. She had been taught from a young age that what she wanted didn't matter. Her people came first. She put everyone before her. Eddie had no problem meeting the needs of her people, but for some strange reason her people wanted to see her mated. She knew it was out of love. They wanted her happy.

She'd finally taken some time away from all of the clan politics, and then fate went and sided with her clan and delivered her life partner practically in her lap.

Eddie carried Liana quickly through the snow back to the cabin. Tremors racked Liana's frame. Eddie's pace increased. She had to get her warm before hypothermia set in. By the time she shouldered the door open, Eddie shook from holding Liana's body.

Warmth from the fire washed over them. Eddie stalked her way to the hearth. She knelt and laid Liana gently on the thick rug. She tugged the soggy boots from Liana's feet, careful not to cause her any pain when it came to her injured ankle. Liana's breath hitched. Eddie couldn't tell if it was from the cold or something else.

"Stay here. Whatever you do, don't go to sleep," she ordered. She rose to her feet. "I'll get you towels and dry clothes."

She vanished down the hall. Her bear slammed into her chest with a force that caused her to stumble into the wall.

Mate.

Eddie shook her head and ignored her beast. Her bear wanted to go back and curl around Liana to allow her heat to help warm her. But there was no way Liana could shift into her bear inside the cabin. At the moment, they had to be sure pneumonia didn't set in for Liana, and getting her out of those soaked clothes was a must. They were unable to leave the cabin due to the amount of snow. She doubted the plow trucks had cleared the road. While shoveling, she hadn't heard one car pass by the entire time she'd been outside.

Eddie grabbed towels from the linen closet. She flew into her room and snagged wool socks, fleece pants, and a long-sleeved shirt for Liana. Eddie's clothes were too big for her, but at least they were dry. She made a mental note go and retrieve Liana's luggage from her car later. For now, Eddie's clothes would have to do again.

Eddie returned to the living room. She eyed the fire and dropped the items in her arms onto the floor next to Liana. She moved swiftly to the fireplace and tossed a couple of logs into the flames. She needed to build the fire up to get the cabin warmer for Liana. She shucked her coat and boots then went back to her.

She knelt by Liana and began stripping the wet clothes off her. It was a struggle to remove her soaked pants and shirt. Eddie tried not to stare at Liana as she removed her panties and bra. Her smooth brown skin was highlighted by the firelight. Her large breasts had the most perfect shape with her dark areolas. Her nipples were tiny hard buds that Eddie ached to take in her mouth. She averted her eyes and continued. This was not the time to ogle this beautiful woman.

Liana didn't protest, but rather, she couldn't with the way she was trembling and her teeth chattering. Eddie took one of the large fluffy towels and wrapped it around her. She tucked the corners underneath her arms. She took another one and wrapped it around her legs and drew a blanket from the pile she had pushed away from the hearth and draped that around Liana as well. She leaned in close and kept her arm around her. The heat from her should help as well.

Liana's head turned to her. Her eyes flicked up. They stared at each other in silence. As much as Eddie wanted to be angry at Liana for not listening, she couldn't find it in herself to not forgive her.

"You scared the hell out of me," Eddie admitted. When she'd heard the scream, she had thought Liana had come under attack. She was a little relieved that it had just been her falling in the creek rather than the rogue wolf assaulting her.

Eddie's bear would have unleashed her power had that been the case. There would have been no stopping the change. Her bear would have wanted blood had a single hair on Liana's head been harmed. The protective nature of her bear was at an all-time high. Her animal was not going to let this woman out of her sight.

"I'm sorry," Liana whispered. "I just wanted to see the creek."

"You should have asked me. You're lucky I heard you. This is Montana in the winter. A few minutes longer and you could be—" Eddie couldn't finish her words. She gave Liana a squeeze and hoped that between the heat from the fire and the warmth from her body, Liana would thaw out.

A shiver rippled through Liana again. "You would have said no."

"I probably would have." Eddie snorted. She pulled Liana closer to her and rested her chin against her temple. She couldn't help but want to start her campaign to get Liana to stay. "There are many beautiful sights to see here in Lurton. When we're not under a storm warning, I could show you around."

If Liana was so intent to see a creek, she

would love the mountains, the open plains, their beautiful town. It didn't matter what season they were in, Montana was always breathtakingly beautiful.

"That would be nice," Liana replied softly. She leaned into Eddie and inhaled sharply. "You are like a furnace. How are you so warm after being outside?"

"It's just my physiology." Eddie shrugged. She reached up and pushed some of Liana's hair that had escaped her braids out of her face. She tucked it behind Liana's small, rounded ear. She was fascinated by the long coiled hair with its golden ends. She would love to see it wild and free along her pillows back home.

Eddie's breathing stopped short. The vision that came to her sent her heart rate skyrocketing. Thankfully, her little mate wasn't a shifter and wouldn't be able to scent her sharp arousal. This woman in her arms certainly did things to her. The brief moment she'd seen Liana's naked breasts were etched in her memory forever. Eddie's core clenched at the scent of her. It was warm and welcoming, even with the tinge of outdoors and the cold. Liana pressed her cold nose to the crook of Eddie's neck.

"Are you warm enough yet?" Eddie's voice was a low, husky whisper.

"Getting there," Liana said. "You definitely help. I love how the heat comes off you."

That was a dangerous answer. Her bear surged forward. She wanted to claim Liana right at this moment.

No. Not now. Liana needs us to keep her warm, Eddie murmured to her beast. The bear had the nerve to grumble before she settled down. Eddie forced a slow exhale and tried keep all carnal thoughts of Liana out of her mind.

"Keep talking to me. Don't fall asleep."

"What do you want to talk about?" Liana laughed.

"Anything."

"You came pretty fast. Like you knew exactly where I was."

"I heard you," Eddie replied. "People may not realize how fast we bears are."

"I'd love to meet your bear one day," Liana said.

Eddie froze and glanced down. She was met with the wide-eyed stare of her intended. Eddie's bear's head rose at the mention of meeting her. She would love that, too. As the mate of an alpha bear, she would be the most protected woman around. Eddie's bear was strong and fierce. She'd faced down plenty of other bears who had challenged her for the title of alpha.

They'd all lost.

Eddie's fingers found their way to Liana's cheek. They were still slightly cold with a rosy tint to them. The fire snapped, sending a flickering flame up the chimney. The wind hissed along the eaves, signaling the second wave of the storm was blowing in.

But all Eddie cared about was Liana.

They were close enough that Eddie could smell the water lingering on Liana, along with the faint sweetness of whatever lotion she'd used. Liana's pupils dilated wide. Eddie trailed her finger down the softness of Liana's face and stopped just below her plump bottom lip.

A lip that she'd had the pleasure to taste, not once, but twice.

"You should rest. We need to make sure to get your core temperature up."

"Maybe...I'm already warm enough," Liana whispered.

A teasing glint appeared in Liana's eyes that took Eddie's breath away. The air in the room grew heavy, laced with attraction between the two of them.

"Liana, you don't know what you're doing," Eddie breathed.

"I think I do," Liana whispered.

Somehow her fingers had found their way to Eddie's wrist. Eddie's breath staggered from Liana's touch. There was no denying the spark between them.

"I'm trying to take care of you."

"I know and I thank you for it." Her eyes shimmered in the firelight.

The large window let the natural light flow into the room, but it was the flicker of the firelight that allowed Eddie to see what was brewing in Liana's eyes. There was something there. Not just an attraction, but trust.

And something deeper.

Eddie cupped Liana's face. Her eyes fluttered shut as she leaned into Eddie's palm as if she'd been waiting for her touch. When those dark bedroom eyes opened again, they held a heat in them that took Eddie's breath away.

Mine, her bear growled.

"Eddie…please…"

Those two words unraveled everything inside

Eddie. She brushed her thumb along the corner of Liana's mouth. "Tell me to stop."

"Why would I do that?"

Eddie leaned closer so their lips were a hair's breadth away from each other. For a suspended heartbeat, neither of them moved.

Then Eddie closed the gap and kissed her.

It was supposed to be gentle. Liana had just been through another traumatizing event. She should go slow.

The kiss was everything but soft and gentle.

Fire surged through Eddie's veins as their mouth's met. Heat, relief, and need all crashed together like two storms colliding. Liana's fingers gripped Eddie's shirt, drawing her closer. The blanket slipped loose around her shoulders. Eddie's arm instinctually draped around Liana's waist and dragged her on top of her. Liana straddled Eddie and wrapped her arms around her neck. The blanket completely fell away, leaving Liana naked in Eddie's arms.

Liana gasped into the kiss, and Eddie took advantage of it to deepen it without thinking. Her lips were hungry with the need to claim. The world outside vanished. A low rumble vibrated her chest as Liana reached down and grabbed the edge of Eddie's thick shirt. She pulled it over Eddie's head and tossed it to the side.

They stared at each other, breathing hard while they took each other in. Liana's pebbled dark nipples demanded Eddie's attention. The woman was perfection sitting on her lap. Her body was made to be worshipped, and Eddie was going to take her time doing just that.

Chapter Six

Liana's body no longer trembled due to the cold. The heat that consumed her couldn't even be blamed on the fire.

It was Eddie.

The woman's amber eyes, her plush lips, and her large hands roaming Liana's body had her feeling as if she was going to combust at any moment. Eddie's gaze was frozen on Liana's breasts. Her breath snagged in her throat; the bear took her all in. She didn't want to move as Eddie's hand came up to palm her soft mound. A low, guttural groan rumbled from Eddie. The sound sent a wave of desire straight to Liana's core.

Liana's nipples hardened to the point they

ached against her palm. Eddie's hand shook when she caressed the beaded bud. Her gaze rose to meet Liana's. Her eyes were filled with a wild hunger.

"Liana..." Eddie groaned. She leaned down and captured the bud with her mouth.

Liana gasped at the hot heat that surrounded her sensitive nipple. She arched into Eddie's hold while she suckled upon Liana.

Another rumble came from Eddie. The sound did something to Liana. She loved hearing it and wanted to feel Eddie unleash her pent-up passion. Eddie's other hand gripped Liana's hip, hard. Liana didn't mind the slight hint of pain. Eddie shifted them so Liana was now lying on her back on the rug. She positioned herself over Liana and gazed down at her.

Eddie's intense stare had Liana's heart racing. Her amber-eyed gaze traveled down the length of her as if she were trying to memorize all of her. Eddie's head lowered slowly, and this time she captured the other nipple with her mouth. Liana moaned and pulled Eddie's hair from her ponytail. She wanted to feel the thick strands. She entwined her fingers in her hair and held on while her mouth took possession of her breast. Liana arched her back upward, unable to hold still.

Eddie released Liana's nipple and blazed a trail of hot kisses along her belly. She moved farther down, her hands sliding along Liana's body. The calluses on her hands sent a shiver through Liana.

"Eddie…" This time it was Liana who moaned Eddie's name.

She widened her legs to open them. Eddie reached her center, paused, and glanced up at Liana. She should have felt open and exposed, maybe even vulnerable, but all Liana felt was alive.

Eddie's amber gaze made her feel wanted… needed…sexy.

Eddie positioned herself between Liana's legs. Her hands clamped down on Liana's thighs and pushed them open wider. Eddie inhaled, and Liana practically unraveled. Was she breathing in her scent? She was a shifter, and they relied on scent for many things she'd learned over the years from her friendship with Terri.

Eddie's eyes darkened to almost black. She inhaled, and that rumble sounded again. Liana's body shook with anticipation of what was to come. Eddie lowered her head and ran her wide tongue over Liana's pussy in one long stroke.

Liana cried out, tightening the fingers in Eddie's hair.

Eddie repeated the move, eliciting another cry of ecstasy. She continued and feasted upon Liana. Her tongue was everywhere. The grip on her thighs tightened to an almost unbearable hold, but Liana ignored it. She was too lost in the feel of Eddie latching on to her clit.

The woman needed no encouragement or coaxing or direction. She knew exactly what she was doing. Her tongue pushed at Liana's entrance before sliding through her slick folds. She returned to sucking on Liana's swollen bud, and her cries filled the air.

Liana was not embarrassed by the sounds she was making. She had a beautiful lover focused on her and her pleasure. Why wouldn't she reward her that she was doing a damn good job?

A single finger slid inside Liana's slick core. Her muscles clamped down on it in a possessive hold. It was withdrawn slightly, then two surged deep inside her. Eddie continued to take possession of her clit, and Liana gasped at the feeling of her channel being stretched.

Liana gasped, and her body trembled. Eddie took what she wanted.

It was hers.

Anything Eddie wanted, Liana would be willing to let her have.

Liana blinked then glanced down at the head between her legs. The sight of Eddie staring at her while she feasted and fucked Liana with her fingers sent a violent tremor through her. Liana's hips moved on their own accord. She held Eddie's gaze and rode her face and fingers.

Her breaths were coming fast. Eddie sucked her harder, introducing a third finger inside Liana. Her long fingers sank in and out in slow, easy strokes.

She took it all.

Liana could barely form a conscious thought. The only things that filled her brain was the pleasure Eddie was wringing from her. She didn't want this moment to end.

Eddie forged her fingers inside Liana and held them still as she hummed and shook her head, clamping down on Liana's clit.

Liana's body detonated.

She came hard and fast. She closed her eyes, intense trembles taking over her body. Eddie didn't let up on her. She continued to suck until Liana could barely breathe. Liana begged and pleaded, but it was to no avail.

Eddie was trying to ruin her.

Destroy her.

When the last shudder calmed down and she lay in a puddle on the floor, Eddie finally released her swollen bud. She lifted her head and gazed down at Liana with a possessive glint in her eye. Her face was wet with the evidence of Liana's release. She licked her lips and withdrew her fingers slightly before allowing them to sink back inside. She held them there and pushed up off the floor.

Liana's muscles felt like wet noodles. She could barely move. Eddie leaned over her and took her lips in a deep kiss. Her tongue swept in, allowing Liana to taste herself. Another moan escaped Liana. Eddie tilted her head to the side. She slowly thrust her fingers inside Liana.

She tore her mouth from Eddie's.

"I can't…" Liana gasped. There was no way Eddie was going to demand another orgasm from her. The one she'd just experienced was so damn hard, and her muscles were weak.

"But you can." Eddie smirked.

Liana grew worried. Would Eddie be disappointed in her if she couldn't reach a second orgasm so quickly after the first one? It usually took a while before she could. Past lovers had tried to get her to have back-to-back orgasms, and most times she would fake it to save their egos.

She would never try to fake anything with Eddie. Liana was sure Eddie would be able to tell the difference between a real one and fake one.

Eddie settled back on her haunches and continued pushing her fingers deep inside. Her thumb drew small circles on her clit. Liana bit her lip at the sensation. Eddie's large hand settled on her breasts and played with it. She held Liana's gaze as she worked her body. Liana's breaths were coming in hard pants.

She couldn't tear her eyes away from Eddie if she tried.

Eddie's hand slammed into her. Over and over, she sent her fingers into Liana's slick channel. She twisted them around and continued her assault. Liana's body jerked. She suddenly felt her muscles tighten to where she couldn't move her legs. She kept them open for Eddie. She didn't want to let her down.

She could do this.

She could reach the stars.

Because Heaven had to be where she was going if she came again.

"This is all mine," Eddie growled. Her amber eyes practically glowed. She watched Liana. Her fangs peeked from underneath her lips.

Liana couldn't tear her gaze away from them. Would Eddie bite her? Claim her?

Would she want her to?

A shudder went through Liana, and warmth ran through her. It settled low in her belly and continued on to her core. Her slickness was in overdrive. She could feel it pour out of her. The sounds of it filled the air with each thrust of Eddie's hand. Liana had never felt anything like this before. Her hips thrust forward, meeting Eddie's fingers, allowing them to go deeper.

A cry was torn from Liana. She turned herself completely over to Eddie who let loose another growl. Liana lost it. Her back arched off the floor, pleasure washing over her. It was harder for her to breathe. She dragged in air, but it didn't feel as if there was any left. Liana felt like the storm that was raging outside was here in the room with them.

Her muscles clenched down around Eddie's fingers as she reached the pinnacle.

A piercing cry broke the silence. Her eyes shut tight, and another orgasm took over her. It wasn't until she tried to suck in another breath of air that she realized the scream was coming from her.

Liana fell back onto the rug, spent, unable to move.

Again.

Her skin was slick and hot. Eddie slowly withdrew her fingers from her pussy. Liana didn't even have the strength to open her eyes. She had to focus on her breathing for fear that she would stop after expending the massive amount of energy that came with reaching a hard orgasm like she just had.

Twice.

Liana stirred beneath the weight of the blankets. Her cheek pressed against the warm wool and the faint scent of wood. For a moment, she didn't know where she was. The only thing she knew was her body felt viciously heavy and her skin tingled in way that had nothing to do with the cold.

Then a chill hit her.

A shiver rippled through her. She tried to burrow down in the blankets, but it was too late. Her eyes snapped open, and everything came rushing back to her. The fire had burned low. There was little more than glowing embers in the hearth. She shivered again and tried to pull the blanket tighter around her. She shifted her body, and her foot brushed against bare skin.

Eddie.

Liana rolled over onto her side to face her new lover. Eddie was tangled in the blankets. Her dark hair spilled over one arm, her face softened by slumber. Even though she was asleep, Eddie still gave off powerful vibes. The woman held a wildness to her that couldn't be hidden.

Liana sighed and watched Eddie.

Everything leading up until this night had been a set of misfortunes. The car accident, almost freezing to death, and then almost drowning.

Yet through all the chaos and danger, Eddie made her feel safe.

Liana's fingers itched to touch Eddie. She wanted to trace along her jawline and down to those magical lips that had pulled multiple orgasms from her.

But she didn't.

Eddie deserved to rest.

So instead, she continued to watch her so she could memorize every detail of the woman she already knew she'd caught feelings for. A sigh escaped Eddie's lips. Her body moved slightly under the blankets. The sound stirred something in Liana.

Affection for this woman.

Something else that was far too dangerous to mention right now.

A piece of wood cracked and popped in the hearth. The chill in the air was getting worse. Liana pulled the blanket tighter again, but it was no use. Her toes were freezing. She was about to reach for another blanket that hadn't made it to the pile that Eddie had put underneath them when Eddie stirred.

"What's wrong? Are you cold?" Eddie asked.

"A little." Liana downplayed it.

Eddie sat up and rubbed her eyes before glancing over at the dying fire.

"I'll fix it," she murmured. She pushed the blankets aside and rose.

Liana's mouth went dry at the sight of Eddie's naked form. Her long, dark hair rested mid back, her ass was sculpted perfectly, and her legs were long and toned. Eddie crouched to add another log to the smoldering fire. Sparks rose in a gentle flare as the new log caught.

Liana's heart thundered against her chest while she watched her poke the embers, coaxing the flames back to life.

"Doesn't look like the lights are coming back on anytime soon," Liana said.

"At least we still have the generator to give us some power." Eddie reached over and grabbed another log and tossed it in the growing fire.

"Do you get outages like this often?"

"Sometimes." Eddie straightened and turned toward her, a faint smile appearing on her lips. "This far up the mountain, it's part of the deal. Winter takes what it wants."

"You sound like you're okay with that." Liana found herself smiling.

Eddie walked back to the pallet she'd made them. She sat and slid underneath the blankets next to Liana.

"After a while, you stop fighting the wild and start listening to it."

The warmth of Eddie's body seeped through immediately, chasing away the cold. For a few heartbeats, neither of them spoke. It was a comfortable silence. The crackle of the fire, the wind outside, and the soft hum of the generator filled the air.

Liana finally broke the silence.

"You never did mention why you are in a cabin secluded away from the world," Liana said.

She scooted closer to Eddie who was lying on her back with her hands folded behind her head. Liana didn't hesitate to sidle in close to her so her head rested in the crook of Eddie's shoulder. Eddie glanced down at her. There was a veil that came over her that Liana couldn't decipher. Had she asked a question she shouldn't?

Eddie remained quiet for a moment before turning her attention back to the ceiling. Liana thought that maybe Eddie wasn't going to answer. It truly wasn't any of her business why Eddie was hidden away from the world.

"I'm the alpha of the Brown Claw Clan. Lurton is my territory," Eddie said.

Liana blinked. That wasn't what she'd expected.

"The alpha? Like the leader of the bear shifters in Lurton?"

"And the surrounding area as well," Eddie replied. She gave a short laughed and exhaled.

"Wow. That sounds…exhausting." Liana sat up and leaned onto her elbow so she could study Eddie more. To be an alpha, she would assume the person would be the strongest of their kind in order to lead.

"You could say that. It's why I'm here. I needed to get away. I haven't had one day to myself in years. Everyone always needs something. Guidance, approval, decisions, protection…which I have to give. It's my duty to take care of and protect every member of my clan. But lately they have become demanding of me in other ways."

Liana couldn't fathom having to be responsible for an entire town of people. She was barely capable of taking care of herself.

"What are they demanding?" Liana whispered.

"A mate." The word came out like it carried too much weight for her, but Eddie was tall, strong, with broad shoulders.

She thought of how Eddie had been adamant on taking care of her since she'd arrived. That just showed how much the woman cared about mankind. She didn't know Liana at all and immediately was there to help in her time of need.

But then Liana processed the word again.

Mate.

"They want you married?" Her stomach twisted at the thought of Eddie with another woman. She swallowed hard before continuing. "Why?"

"The clan thinks I need one. Someone to balance me. Keep the peace. Continue the line, all that traditional stuff."

"What do you think about it?" Liana asked quietly.

"I believe in fate, and she knows what is best. I am not going to let someone else decide who that should be." There was a hardness to Eddie's tone.

Liana pitied whoever tried to convince Eddie of anything other than what she believed.

Liana bit her lip, unsure what to say. Shifter politics was not something she was well versed on. She knew a little thanks to Terri, but that was all she knew. No wonder Eddie knew who Terri was. She was the alpha of Terri's clan.

The idea of Eddie belonging to someone else —touching another woman, smiling at her the way she smiled at Liana—made something flare in her chest. But she didn't say anything. She didn't have any right to feel that way.

"Seems to me you deserve someone who sees you, not just the title," Liana said.

Eddie's head turned in her direction. The alpha's amber eyes glowed from the firelight. The wood in the fire crackled, breaking the silence.

"And what about you, Liana? What do you deserve?"

"Not sure. Still trying to figure it out." And that was the truth. She had no idea what she wanted out of life. She had assumed that one day she would settle down with someone. Have a few kids. But lately, nothing had come to fruition.

"Fair enough." Eddie's mouth twitched.

Liana returned to her position in the crook of Eddie's arm. Eddie brought her arm down and enclosed it around Liana, bringing her body flush to hers. There was something special between them. Liana felt it, but she wasn't sure if Eddie did. She snuggled closer and realized she liked the way Eddie looked at her.

It was more than the sex. It was a deep feeling inside her that she couldn't shake—the feeling that something irreversible had started between them. She felt herself drift back off. The warmth of Eddie allowed her to relax again. One question continued to remain in her head.

Did Eddie feel it, too?

Chapter Seven

The storm had left the world wrapped in white silence. Eddie stood on the porch, her breath ghosting in the brittle morning air while the weight of the winter pressed against her lungs. The snow had come heavy through the night. She surveyed the bulky drifts clinging to the cabin's eaves. Snow had swallowed the narrow path she'd shoveled yesterday. The trees bowed beneath the weight of it.

All of it was beautiful in a cruel Montana way. The landscape made her feel small, humbled even. She'd grown up in this kind of wild, but some mornings still left her in awe.

She tugged on her gloves, the leather creaking as she flexed her hands. The generator still hummed behind the cabin. It was half-buried under another fresh coat of snow. She'd have to dig it out again, check the fuel line, and chop more wood before the next wave hit. The scent in the air told her the storm wasn't finished.

She stepped off the porch and sank nearly to her knees.

"Damn," she muttered. The storm had packed the snow tight. It would take hours to clear the truck. Maybe days if Mother Nature continued to dump on them.

She should be frustrated. She'd come here for solitude, not survival mode. She trudged through the snow and tried to concentrate on everything she needed to do, but her thoughts were on a certain person who was inside underneath the blankets and warm.

Liana.

The name caused her heart to flutter.

Eddie had never met anyone like her. She was a city-born woman who was stubborn yet fragile. She made Eddie want to wrap her up and never let her go. Liana tested Eddie in a way that made her bear want to claim her. She was brave, defiant, and curious, all traits that would make a great alpha mate. Even after everything that had happened, she'd laughed that morning as she'd cleaned up the kitchen. Her jovial humming had brought a smile to Eddie's lips.

Mine, her bear grumbled.

She grabbed a shovel that rested against the house and stabbed it into a snowbank with more force than necessary.

"We haven't claimed her yet," Eddie muttered. The thought of marking Liana as hers, keeping her forever, presenting her to the world as her mate, gave her a warm rush of feelings.

Her bear growled low, unhappy with Eddie. The beast couldn't understand the wait. She didn't care about logic, or timing, or anything other than the claiming. There was a pull to be with Liana. Eddie felt it all the way to her soul. Every time Liana looked at her, every time her scent hit the air, Eddie wanted to nuzzle her neck and breathe her in. It had taken everything she had to untangle her limbs from Liana. She had been warm, scented of wild honey and something that made Eddie's pulse spike.

She tried to focus on the work at hand.

One shovel of snow.

Then another.

The rhythmic scrape of metal against the ice underneath the mountains of snow steadied her breathing. Her muscles strained with the weight of the heavy mounds. It felt good to do some physical labor while breathing in the crisp mountain air. The clouds were already thickening again. They were iron gray, pressing low over the tree line. She could almost taste the next wave of snow in the air.

She should leave the snow where it was, but if she did, then it would only be taller and heavier come tomorrow. Plus she needed a distraction.

If she stayed in the cabin all day with Liana, there would only be one physical activity they would be engaged in. She paused and allowed the memory of her face buried between Liana's legs come to the forefront.

The taste of her was addictive. She had been sweet, tangy, and hot. A low rumble from her bear sounded as Eddie's breathing hitched.

Liana's whimpers and cries had filled the cabin. Eddie's tongue had been everywhere. She had wanted to consume all of Liana. She could have stayed there forever in her own little heaven between her woman's thighs. If she closed her eyes, she could still taste a hint of Liana on her tongue.

The door opened behind her. Eddie blinked and turned to find Liana standing bundled up in one of Eddie's thick hoodies and an oversized coat that probably belonged to one of Eddie's cousins. It was long enough that the hem went past Liana's knees. She must have done something to her hair while Eddie had been working. Her curls were wild and free, creating a soft halo around her face, the wind blowing it gently.

Eddie's heart stuttered as she took in Liana's beauty.

"Hey," Liana said. She gave a little wave. She stepped out onto the back porch. She wrapped a scarf around her neck. "You've been out here for a while. Thought you might like some company."

"There's a lot to do before the next storm blows in." Eddie wiped her glove against her forehead.

Her gaze didn't leave Liana who stepped farther onto the porch. The boards creaked under her boots.

"It's stunning out here."

Eddie followed her gaze. There was an

endless sea of white. The only color came from the dark firs and the faint shimmer of the creek in the distance.

"Yeah. When it's not trying to kill you."

That made Liana laugh. "You don't sugar-coat anything, do you?"

"No. I believe in being up front and honest."

Liana glanced over at her. There was a hesitation in her expression that caused Eddie to be curious as to what was running through her head.

"Eddie, I was just thinking. My phone is still in my car, and my bag. I probably need to go and check in on my car. I'm sure it's snowed in, but my sister's probably losing her mind right now."

Eddie's gut tightened. She'd been expecting Liana to bring up her car. She blew out a deep breath. She should have thought of asking Liana if there was anything in the car that she needed, but she had been rushing and trying to get her to safety.

"That road is probably covered under a good three feet of snow. You're not getting near that car without a snowmobile, and I don't have one with me."

"I know," Liana breathed. "I'm not saying I'll

go alone. But maybe later today? Can we try? It's just…I need to at least try. I don't want Jorrie calling in a search party because she hasn't heard from me. Or Terri for that matter. I was supposed to be at her home and I didn't show up."

She wouldn't want Liana's sister and friend becoming worried. Liana was safe, but they wouldn't know that. She glanced in the direction of the road and knew the only possible way of making it to the car would be in her bear form. Her beast would be much faster, and she would be able to handle the terrain.

"I'll go. Once I've checked the rest of the property. You stay here where it's warm."

Liana's mouth pressed into a stubborn line. A gust of wind blew, causing her hair to cover her face. She brushed it aside and shook her head. "I just hate sitting around not doing anything. I've cleaned the kitchen, straightened up the cabin, and I'm one step away from reorganizing your pantry. Let me help with something. I'll go with you."

"You can't. Not with that ankle. You'd slow me down."

"It's fine. The wrap is holding. See?" Liana

raised her leg to show off the wrap that Eddie had redone before she'd come outside.

"Liana." Eddie stepped closer, her voice dropping low. This woman needed to understand that she was trying to keep her safe. Why didn't she get it? "You nearly froze to death. Twice. I'm not about to risk that again."

Liana's expression softened. She nodded after a moment.

"Okay, but only because you look like you're about to throw me over your shoulder if I argue."

"Don't temp me."

That earned a laugh from Liana. Eddie gripped the handle of the shovel tight. The fantasy of tossing her woman over her shoulder and carrying her into the house almost had her moving, but she fought to remain where she stood.

"Now go back inside where it is warm. I promise I won't be out here much longer."

Liana studied her before she gave a small smile. "Okay."

She went back into the cabin. The door shut gently behind her. The porch felt emptier without her there. Eddie turned back to the yard.

The snow glittered under the weak sunlight that peeked through the clouds. Every sound was magnified—the distant groan of tree limbs shifting under the burden of snow, the drip of melting water from the eaves.

And then beneath it all, a whisper.

Eddie's entire body went still. She listened, and there it was again. She tilted her head back slightly and inhaled deep.

A scent.

Wolf.

It was faint but distinct. A muskiness threaded with something off, something feral. Eddie's jaw clenched tight. That was the same scent she had caught when she'd rescued Liana from the creek. She set the shovel aside and scanned the edge of the woods.

Eddie stalked her way through the thick snow back to the creek in the woods. The scent grew stronger. She bit back a growl as her gaze landed on a set of tracks near the creek. They were fresh and half-buried but unmistakable. Wide paws, too large for a regular wolf.

She released that pent-up growl. It was low and carried through the air. This was her territory. Her family's land. And no rogue wolf had any business stalking this close to her cabin or her mate.

She followed the trail a few steps into the trees. She allowed her bear to rise to the surface. Her breath was slow and steady. The prints weaved along the creek's edge, leading deeper into the forest. It had been a least a few hours since the animal had come this way.

The idea that the feral beast had been watching them while they had slept set Eddie's bear on edge. She knelt and pressed her fingers to one of the prints. It was deep and heavy. A male.

"You've made a mistake, wolf," she murmured. Her bear surged forward, demanding to be released. Her animal promised violence if they ever came across the wolf. This was too close to their domain. Too close to their mate.

Her bear was in protective mode, as was Eddie. She would be ready to defend Liana at all costs.

She lingered in the area to scan and scent… but ultimately waiting. Would the wolf come back? She tried to inhale again to see if she could catch its scent, but the wind shifted, blowing down the mountain and carrying any trace of the wolf away.

She trudged back to the cabin. Tension was still coiled in every muscle. She needed to remain calm. She didn't want to go inside and have Liana see her like this. By the time she'd made her way back to the yard again, the snow had started to fall. Big, fat lazy flakes at first, then thicker and faster.

She would have to work quickly to get everything she needed done. She hurried over to the generator and cleared away the snow. Everything looked to be working as it should. She breathed a sigh of relief that it was holding up. There was still the matter of the wood that needed to be split. She wasn't in danger of running out yet, but she had wanted to split more so it could dry out on the porch with the rest.

She had lost track of time chopping the wood. Once she was done, she breathed a sigh of relief. She stacked the last of it on the porch and felt like she'd really accomplished something today. She glanced at the sky and saw those dark clouds were moving in fast.

What do you think about it?

Liana's words echoed in her mind. She

hadn't known how to answer at first. So she'd kept it safe and brought up fate. But she didn't go into how she believed fate had brought the two of them together, or how she believed that Liana was her fated life companion. She'd remained silent on that and kept her answer generic.

What she felt for Liana would probably scare her. She was human, and Eddie didn't know if she truly understood how mating worked. Yes, she was friends with Terri, a member of her clan, but that didn't mean she truly understood what it would mean to be the fated partner of a bear.

Or an alpha bear's consort.

Everything about Liana screamed *mate*. From the way she smiled at Eddie, to the way she'd made the cabin feel less like a refuge and more like a home.

Eddie sighed and pushed her damp hair from her face. She needed to get back inside before the snowfall got worse. She had made Liana a promise and she'd honor that. She'd ensured Liana was safe in the cabin and then shift and go to her car to gather her items.

Eddie reached for the door handle and froze.

The cabin was quiet.

Too damn quiet.

She snatched the door open and stalked inside. The fire still burned in the hearth; the blankets were folded neatly on the couch. The air was colder now, and the faint scent of Liana was still fresh—near the front door.

Her boots were gone, as was the coat she'd been wearing.

"Liana?" she called out, but she already knew there would be no answer.

Eddie's pulse stumbled, then kicked into overdrive. She raced out the front door and paused. Her gaze swept over the yard. The snow was falling harder now and covering everything. No sound but the wind and her own breath.

A single set of footprints led away from the cabin.

Small, light, and headed in the direction of the road.

Eddie's heart dropped.

"Dammit, Liana!"

Eddie's bear roared. They would need to go after their mate.

Chapter Eight

The cabin door shut behind her with a soft thud. The sound was nearly swallowed by the gust of wind. For a moment, Liana hesitated on the front porch of the cabin. Her gloved hands gripped the railing as she took in the swirling whiteness before her. Snow drifted down in a slow hypnotic spiral. She inhaled sharply. The world had been reduced to a blinding blur of silver and gray.

She should go back inside.

She knew that.

But her stomach twisted with a different kind of unease. It wasn't fear but restlessness.

Guilt.

Eddie had been working all day from the moment she'd woken up. She'd shoveled, chopped wood, fixed a few things out in the yard, getting them ready for whatever was to come. Everything she did appeared to be deliberate and efficient. The woman was capable of taking care of them.

And Liana? What had she been doing while the alpha had been out in the cold working?

She'd cleaned the kitchen. Dusted a house that didn't have a speck of dust. Straightened up the bathroom and living room. All of which had taken a little over an hour.

Liana wanted to help. To contribute. To matter in this place that wasn't her world. She just wasn't used to someone taking care of her. She'd been on her own and providing for herself since she had graduated from college. Her parents had raised her to be self-sufficient. So to have someone literally do everything for her—drove her crazy.

Her gaze turned toward the direction of the buried road. Somewhere down that slope, under layers of snow, would be her car waiting for her. Her phone, her tablet, her chargers—everything she owned that connected her to the outside world—was locked inside that vehicle.

What if something happened?

There wasn't a phone in the cabin. Eddie had said it proudly like it was a badge of honor to be completely disconnected from the world.

No signal. No service. No interruptions.

Apparently, she was determined to take a break from her clan. The beta had been put in charge while she had taken some time away.

But again, what if something happened and they needed help? Liana was even more determined to go after her phone and charger. The wind bit through the scarf she'd borrowed. Due to her dunk in the creek, she was unable to wear her coat. It was still wet. When she'd been going through the cabin, she'd found additional clothing and outwear. Whoever the coat belonged to must be a giant. It practically dwarfed her.

Her boot sank in the drift. The cold nipped at her cheeks immediately.

"I'll be fine. It's not that far," she whispered to herself. She remembered the trek when Eddie had rescued her. They had arrived at the cabin in no time. She blew out a deep breath that puffed into the air as a white cloud. The snow was deeper than she'd thought. She took another step, and this time she sank down to her knees.

Each step was work. It was a battle between her stubbornness and the snow.

Eddie's warning replayed in her mind.

That road is probably covered under a good three feet of snow. You're not getting near that car without a snowmobile.

But Liana had grown up in Colorado winters. She wasn't some delicate flower. She could handle a ton of snow.

Right?

She kept her focus on the faint line of dark pines ahead, her guess at the direction of where the street was located. The wind howled and threw some snow against her. The first flicker of doubt that entered her mind was when she glanced back. The cabin was gone, swallowed by the flurries of snow. There was only whiteness behind her.

Her stomach dropped.

Okay...maybe it's a little farther than I thought, she told herself. She forced her legs to continue moving. She tried to go faster, but with the amount of snow she was trudging through, she was probably going the same speed, if not slower.

"Just a bit more. I'm sure I'll see the car any second now," she muttered.

A few more minutes or maybe an hour passed. Nothing.

She didn't see anything but snow. Endless, swirling snow.

The cold had definitely set into her. She didn't feel any pain anymore when it came to her ankle. The throbbing she had been used to feeling had dulled until she could barely feel it. She tried to convince herself that it was a good thing. Maybe she was getting used to the cold.

Except she wasn't.

Halfway through another drift, she stumbled and caught herself on one knee. Her breath came out ragged through the scarf.

"This is not the time to be falling." She chuckled. Not that she found any of this funny. She closed her eyes and breathed in and had to focus. She refused to be like one of those characters in a horror movie. "There's no one chasing you. Take your time. Keep going."

She stood and stretched. It couldn't be much longer. It hadn't taken Eddie long to make it from the crash site to the cabin.

Something cracked in the distance. A sharp, clean snap.

Liana froze as her heart skipped a beat. Her gaze swept across the area near her, but she didn't see anything.

"Eddie?" she called out. She raised her voice against the wind. "Eddie, is that you?"

Silence.

The wind shrieked, and she almost jumped out of her skin. For a moment, she thought she'd heard something else woven into the sound. Like an animal, but it sounded wrong. Her pulse spiked.

It's just the wind and my imagination, she tried to convince herself. She pushed forward and continued on. She had to fight to keep her footsteps steady and even. She tried to keep her mind on something else—anything but the potential of a wild animal stalking her.

Of course, her thoughts went to Eddie.

The feeling of her strong body pressed to Liana's.

The way Eddie's voice changed when she'd whispered her name in her ear this morning to awaken her.

The way she'd touched her. Made love to her. Protected her.

Was Eddie truly real? Had all of this been a fantasy and she had just been wandering along, lost, ever since the crash?

A tear slipped down her cheek and froze almost instantly. No, she knew Eddie was very much real. There was no way that the universe would be so cruel as to make everything she'd experienced with Eddie be a fantasy.

Liana didn't want to die out here. Not like this. Not when she'd found a woman who cared for her and made her feel alive.

The storm thickened. Flakes flew into her face, making it harder for her to see. She hunched deeper into her coat, one gloved hand shielding her eyes. The snow came in sideways now, a curtain of white noise. Her sense of direction vanished completely.

She had no idea where she was and if she was even headed in the right direction.

"Okay, girl. You got this. Just turn around and retrace your steps. The cabin is warm and waiting for you. Eddie won't even know you've been gone." She was trying to stay calm and not lose her shit. She spun around and glanced down. The bottom of her stomach gave way.

The wind had erased her tracks. Every mark of her boots was gone.

"Well, fuck."

Panic clawed up her throat. She turned in a slow circle, trying to seek any landmark that would help her. She squinted to see if she might catch the silhouette of the cabin, but the world looked the same in every direction.

White, white, and then more white.

Her breaths came faster now. She tightened her scarf and tried to keep moving. The reasoning that the car had to be somewhere near kept her going. But the cold was starting to steal her thoughts. They drifted like the snow, surrounding her and landing everywhere.

She remembered the warmth of Eddie's arms, the roughness of her palms on her soft skin. The languid rumble of her growl. The quietness of her in the aftermath of their love-making when she'd rested her head on Eddie and listened to her heartbeat slow down. The world had certainly felt safer then.

That memory was a lifeline. It kept her going. She would make it back to Eddie. She was one determined woman, and if she knew anything, she would survive this.

"I'll be fine," she whispered. Her lips were beginning to feel numb. "Eddie will be pissed, but I'll be fine."

Her eyes stung from the wind. Her fingers burned under the gloves. She tried to keep her mind busy. She counted her steps, named all of the colors that she did see, but the howling of the wind in her ears drowned out everything.

Then came another sound.

A distant, guttural howl.

Liana froze. Her blood ran cold. This time it wasn't the wind. That was surely a live animal. She turned sharply and scanned around her. The sound echoed again. This time it was closer, threading through the trees.

"Eddie?" she called out. Her voice cracked as panic took over. "Please!"

Nothing answered but the wind.

Her heart hammered against her chest so hard she could feel it all the way in to her fingertips. She stumbled forward, half running, half falling. She had to find the car. Had to find some kind of shelter. The snow blurred her vision, her lashes heavy with ice.

Shapes formed off in the distance. Her breath caught. The road. She was sure of it. She could see a faint dip in the landscape where the road must be buried.

And there was a darker shadow. The outline of something—her car! It had to be.

Relief flooded her so fast she almost sobbed.

"Yes," she gasped. She dragged herself through the snow toward the car. "Finally!"

The howl came again.

Closer.

Terror gripped her. Liana didn't dare look back. Every instinct screamed for her to move. She half ran, half crawled. The snow was up to her thighs now. Her ankle screamed, but she barely felt it. Her lungs burned. She didn't care.

Her fingers, stiff and clumsy from the cold, brushed the frozen metal of the driver's door. She could have cried.

She yanked on the handle. It didn't budge. Ice crusted over the edges, sealing it tight.

"No, no, no." She tugged harder, pounding her fist on the frame until pain shot up her arm. The handle finally gave a little, but it still wouldn't open. The cold had welded it shut.

She leaned her forehead on the window. Her

breaths were coming in hard pants, and she fought the dizzying blur in her vision. Her reflection stared back at her. Her lips were dark, her lashes thick with ice, and there was nothing but fear in her eyes. She wasn't going to die here. Not when she'd come this far.

Her head snapped up at a howl that was too close to comfort. Her breath fogged the glass as she peered through the frost. And then she saw it. A shape creeping through the storm. Dark fur, massive shoulders, eyes that caught what little light there was and gleamed like embers.

A wolf.

Huge and wild, and somehow it looked wrong.

Her body locked up, breath frozen in her chest. The thing was watching her. Studying her.

"No," she whispered.

This had to be the feral wolf that Eddie had told her about. This was no ordinary wolf. It took another step in her direction. She fumbled for the door handle again. Her gloves slipped. She ripped them off and ignored the burn of the cold against her bare skin and yanked with everything she had. The door groaned, ice cracking around the seal, and finally gave.

She threw herself inside and slammed it shut behind her. She hit the lock, her hands shaking. The air inside the car was frigid. Her breath floated in the dim light like mist. She curled up in the seat, shivering and trying not to make a sound. The silence pressed in around her.

Then came the crunch of snow.

Liana turned her head slowly toward the windshield. Through the patch of glass not covered by snow, she could see it. The wolf. It stood in front of the car. Steam rose from its breath in the icy air. Its fur was dark, matted, and the shoulders rippled as it prowled. Its eyes were locked on her.

It stalked closer one step at a time. It circled the vehicle. It brushed the side, and the car shook slightly. It dragged its claws along the side of the car, damaging the metal.

Liana pressed back in the seat, every nerve screaming, her pulse pounding in her throat.

"Eddie," she whispered.

The wolf stopped in front of the car. It lifted its head and howled.

The sound tore through the storm. It was wild, guttural, and tortuous.

Liana clamped her hands over her ears. She

trembled, and her eyes burned with a new set of tears. She couldn't move. Couldn't think. All she could do was pray that somewhere out there, Eddie had heard the howl—and her prayer.

The wolf lowered its head again and paced slowly through the snow. It was waiting. Watching.

Liana sat alone in the freezing dark, her breath fogging up the glass. The only response to the wolf was the wind. She closed her eyes and prayed that Eddie would come to her rescue.

Chapter Nine

The snow was relentless. Thick white flakes hurled sideways as if the wind had lost its mind. Eddie stood on the front porch with her eyes narrowed at the swirling storm. Her chest burned from chopping wood, her muscles were coiled, but that wasn't what had her jaw locked tight.

It was the sight of Liana's footprints—half filled, half frozen, leading away from the cabin.

Eddie cursed under her breath. Her bear prowled beneath her skin. It paced and snarled. Their mate was out there in this mess. For what? A phone that was probably dead. A few clothes? Her stubborn, beautiful, and reckless human didn't understand the danger these mountains held.

Eddie pulled her coat shut, but it did little to ease the heat rising inside her. She stepped off the porch with the snow crunching beneath her boots. The cold bit into her face instantly, but her bear's blood kept her warm enough to move without hesitation.

She followed the trail down the slope toward the tree line. The storm was growing heavier by the minute. Visibility was shrinking fast. The scent of Liana lingered—soft, sweet, and tinged with the faint metallic sting of fear. Eddie's gut twisted.

"Why would she not listen to me?" she growled.

Her boot sank deep. The world had turned into a blur of white and gray shadows. The wind shrieked through the pines like warning cries. The farther she went, the weaker Liana's scent became scattered by the storm.

Then she heard it.

A howl. Low. Long. Wrong.

Every muscle Eddie's body grew taut. That wasn't the call of a wolf pack. It wasn't any pack that she knew. This was something else. Something broken.

Her bear roared inside her chest. The sound vibrated through her bones. She didn't think or hesitate. She tore off her coat and gloves and dropped them onto the ground. The shift rippled through her like wildfire. Her tendons snapped and reshaped. Her bones expanded and thickened. Her body stretched, and her skin disappeared underneath a wave of golden-brown fur, until Eddie the human was gone and in her place stood a ferocious grizzly.

Eight feet of raw fury.

Her breath steamed in the freezing air. Her talons dug trenches in the snow. Her nostrils flared—and there it was. Liana. Her scent, faint but distinct.

And the wolf.

A snarl ripped from her throat as she barreled forward. The snow exploded around her with each stride. The storm clawed at her, but she didn't slow. Her heart pounded with a single instinct.

Protect their mate.

The tracks twisted through the trees, toward the old forest road. Eddie crashed through the drifts, branches snapping under her weight. Then she saw it. The shape of Liana's car half-buried and the shadow that circled it.

The wolf.

It was massive, its pelt a patchwork of matted gray. It's eyes were a wild, sickly yellow. This was no sane creature. It reeked of rot and bloodlust.

Eddie let out a thunderous roar that shook the air. The wolf turned and snarled at her. It set its sights on Eddie. That was what she wanted. She didn't see Liana, but going by the misted windows, assumed she was inside the vehicle.

The wolf faced her, then lunged.

They collided with a sound that split the storm. It was a clash of beasts, teeth and claws. Eddie's weight sent them both tumbling into the snow. Her massive paws struck the wolf. She knocked the wolf down, but it jumped right up and lunged at her again. It snapped at Eddie's throat, and she slammed it down to the ground. The snow flew into the air around them.

She bit down on its shoulder. The fur and flesh gave way beneath her jaws. The wolf howled, twisted, and tried to rake her belly with its claws. Eddie was the stronger of the two.

She was an alpha.

Her bear was in charge, but Eddie was still in the background. Her bear growled and refused to let the wolf go.

Mate. Our mate. You die, her bear roared.

The fight was brutal and primal. The snow turned crimson beneath them. The wolf writhed, screeched, but Eddie's rage didn't waver. She fought with purpose—love.

And that made her unstoppable.

She hurled the creature, sending it crashing against a tree. It landed hard and struggled to rise. It fled into the forest, disappearing into the white blur of the storm.

Eddie stood there with her chest heaving, her sides streaked with blood that wasn't all hers. Her talons flexed, but the bear's fury subsided as the new scent hit her.

Liana's fear.

She turned toward the car. Through the slush and shattered snow, she could see movement. A brown face behind the windshield.

Liana.

Her mate.

Her heart thudded painfully.

Eddie fell down on all fours and lumbered toward the car until she reached the driver's side.

She could smell Laina's panic. The sharp tang of adrenaline mixed with cold and tears.

Slowly, she stepped back and forced herself to calm down. Her body trembled as she shifted. Her bones ground together, and fur pulled back into flesh until she stood naked and human again. Steam rose from her skin in the frigid temperatures. She pressed a hand to the window.

"Liana," she said. She cleared her throat. The sound of her voice was rough. "It's me."

Liana's eyes were wild with shock, then relief filled them.

Eddie yanked on the frozen handle. Her muscles strained until it gave. The door flew open with a groan, and the rush of icy air hit them. Liana's body trembled in the driver's seat. She reached over and grabbed a bag and tossed items in it. She frantically gathered the things she'd come for. Eddie watched her and had to bite back the words that were on the tip of her tongue.

"Eddie," Liana gasped. "It was out there——"

"I know," Eddie said. Her voice was firm but trembled. She crouched and scooped Liana up without another word. Her skin burned against the freezing air, but she didn't care. She could feel how cold Liana was. How close she'd come to real danger.

She held Liana tight to her chest. Liana buried her face against Eddie's neck.

"I just wanted—"

"Don't," Eddie interjected. Her voice was low and sharp. "Not right now."

The wind howled louder as the snow bit at her bare skin. She turned and trudged back toward the cabin. Each step was heavy. The weight of her anger matched the storm around them.

Her mate was safe and alive.

But her fury scorched through the relief like acid. She'd nearly lost her—again.

The snow charred Eddie's bare skin like fire, but she didn't slow. Liana's shivering form was clutched tightly to her chest, her heartbeat racing rapidly. Eddie's strides ate up the distance, her breath forming thick clouds in the frozen air.

By the time the cabin came into view, its outline blurred by the storm, her legs ached and her lungs stung from the cold. The world was pure silence and white fury with only the gentle hum of the generator breaking up the monotony.

She climbed the porch steps in two strides and kicked the door open with her bare foot. Warm air hit her like a sigh of relief. Inside, she lowered Liana carefully onto the thick rug in front of the hearth.

A sense of déjà vu overtook her.

The fire had dimmed to glowing embers. She moved over to it and fed it a few logs and tried to coax the flames back to life. Within a few minutes, the fire roared and bathed the room in light and warmth.

"Eddie, I—"

"Don't," Eddie rasped. She stood and watched the flames. She didn't look at her. She couldn't. "You could have died out there. Again."

Silence blanketed the room.

Eddie drew in a deep breath and tried to contain the storm that raged inside her. She turned sharply and disappeared down the small hallway. She had to force herself to move, to do something instead of exploding.

She stepped into the bathroom and went over to the tub. She ran the water until steam rose. The generator powered the heater that fed the pipes. She leaned against the sink and gripped the porcelain, her knuckles going white.

Her reflection in the mirror was a stranger. Wild-eyed, streaked with dirt and blood. Her hair was a tangled mess from the shift. Her bear still clawed beneath the surface, restless and unsettled.

"You almost lost her," she whispered. "Again."

Her throat burned. She closed her eyes and forced a slow exhale through her lips. She had been careless. She should have kept a closer eye on Liana. Explained the dangers of the wild to her, warned her again about the wolf she'd spotted.

Maybe she should have stopped what she was doing when Liana had come outside and gone immediately to the car to gather her belongings. If she had, Liana wouldn't have taken it upon herself to go and try to retrieve her things.

She opened her eyes and stared at her refection. She would have to speak with Liana about all of the dangers that would follow her as the mate of an alpha.

Her hands shook as she went over to the tub and turned off the water. She went to fetch clean towels and placed them on the vanity. When she returned to the living room, Liana was sitting up with a blanket wrapped around her. She stared into the flames, but Eddie wasn't sure she was truly seeing them.

Eddie's heart skipped a beat.

Without a word, she knelt beside her. She scanned Liana for any signs of injury.

"Are you hurt?" she asked. The words were tight and clipped.

Liana shook her head. "No. Just cold."

She didn't offer to help her up. She couldn't. Not yet. The sight of her, afraid and almost frozen in that car, had carved something deep and raw inside her. She didn't trust herself to touch her without breaking down completely.

But then Liana tried to stand and winced. Eddie's restraint crumbled.

"Easy," she murmured. She slipped an arm around her and helped her stand. She took the bulk of Liana's weight when she leaned into her. "I'll need to recheck that ankle."

They slowly made their way into the bathroom. Liana stole glances at Eddie when she thought she wasn't paying attention.

"I'm sorry," Liana whispered.

Eddie froze for a moment. The apology shouldn't have mattered, but it did. Liana just didn't understand what Eddie had gone through when she'd thought she would lose her. What if she had been too late and the wolf was able to get to her? What if she had continued chopping more wood as she had wanted to? Or went to dig out her truck and bring it out of the garage to get it started?

She didn't want to think of all of the what-ifs, but they kept coming.

Eddie was an alpha bear. It was in her nature to protect, but how was she failing to keep safe the one person fate had deemed for her? How would her clan react at knowing her recent failures?

"I know you are," she said quietly. She helped Liana to the edge of the oversized claw-foot tub. It had been specially made for her family. When the cabin was constructed, her grandmother had demanded a tub large enough for her to soak in comfortably. She'd gotten her wish. "But that doesn't mean you won't do something reckless again."

Maybe Liana was truly a test from fate. She eyed the woman before her, and in her heart she knew she was hers.

Mate, her bear growled.

"You make it sound like I make it a bad habit." Liana's lips quirked. She studied Eddie. "I knew halfway to the car that I had made a mistake. I wanted to come back here, but I couldn't see my tracks anymore."

"Don't," Eddie muttered. She closed her eyes briefly before they opened again. She didn't want to know all the details that would drive her bear crazy and make her feel guilty about not being there for her. "Here. Get in the tub so you can be warmed."

"But what about you? Don't you need to be warmed?"

Eddie's body temperature had dropped for a short time, but now she was back to her normal self. She no longer felt the cold or the chill.

"I'll be fine."

"Get in with me." Liana stared at her with those large brown eyes.

There was something in them that Eddie couldn't read.

"I better not." Eddie shook her head. She was still too unstable emotionally at the moment.

"You're mad at me. I know, but I didn't think—"

"You don't need to think," Eddie interjected.

Her voice came out rougher than she'd intended. She ran a hand along her face and grimaced at the dirt and blood that came away on her palm. She glanced back at Liana. "You just need to trust me."

"But I do trust you." Liana's eyes glistened with unshed tears. She stood and took a step toward Eddie. She paused at Eddie's raised hand. A tear trailed down her cheek.

"Then stop risking yourself. I can't—" Eddie's words faltered. Her throat constricted on the words that needed to come out, but here she was, too damn afraid to really say what she meant. Would Liana accept her? An alpha bear who had failed twice at keeping her safe? She blinked and drew on the strength of her animal. She might as well find out today. "I can't lose you."

That was the honest truth.

Liana closed the gap between them. She rested her hands on Eddie's waist as she tilted her head back so she could meet Eddie's gaze.

"Eddie," she whispered.

She cocked her head to the side slightly. Her dark hair was matted to her scalp, there a smudge of dirt on her cheek, her fingertips were still icy cold, but she was still the most beautiful woman Eddie had ever seen.

"What are we?" Liana asked.

Eddie looked at her—really looked at Liana. Her gaze held a curiosity to it. This was her human. Her mate. The woman who fate had literally dropped into her arms.

"You're mine," she said simply. It was a promise. A vow. A declaration. "And I'm yours. Whether you know what that means or not."

Liana stared at her with wide eyes. Her lips parted, and a sigh escaped her. The air thickened around them. It was charged with something deep and unspoken.

"Take a bath with me. Please." Liana leaned into Eddie. She reached up and guided Eddie's face down to hers. She placed a chaste kiss on her lips. "Your mate is asking this of you."

Eddie's heart stuttered at the use of the word *mate*. Her bear roared inside her and slammed against her chest. Eddie stared at Liana with wide eyes. Did she just accept that she was her mate?

Liana stepped back, away from her, and stripped her clothing from her. She dropped each item onto the floor. She bent down and removed the wrap that had been barely holding on to her ankle. She maintained eye contact with Eddie, revealing her naked form to her. Eddie's mouth grew dry at the sight of Liana's large breasts, her dark areolas, her tapered waist, and rounded hips. Her smooth brown skin glowed in the low light of the room. She backed up and motioned for Eddie to come to her.

Eddie's feet moved on autopilot. There was no way she would be able to refuse such a request from this woman. Eddie took her hand and helped Liana into the tub before she followed in behind her. She sat with Liana in front of her. The warm water surrounded them. It felt damn good, but not as good as Liana saying aloud that she was Eddie's mate.

"What did you call yourself?" Eddie rasped.

Liana's lips curled up in the corner as she looked over her shoulder at Eddie. She turned around in the tub and straddled Eddie's lap. Her knees rested along the side of Eddie's hips. Eddie's hands immediately went to cup Liana's ample bottom in her hand.

Liana reached over to the small table beside the tub and picked up the washcloth and soap. She dipped them in the water and lathered the soap with the cloth. She dropped the soap back in the dish and turned to Eddie.

"Mate." Liana slowly ran the cloth along Eddie's neck and shoulders.

Eddie's bear practically purred at the sound of the word coming from Liana's lips.

Her body shook at Liana taking her time in bathing her. She couldn't find it in her to move. She allowed her to take care of her for once. Was that what a mating required? Eddie's thoughts raced. She couldn't tear her gaze from Liana's face. She appeared to take pleasure in washing her.

Eddie's bear craved to be the one to protect Liana, and care for her, but maybe she was to take care of them, too. She rested her hands on the edge of the tub. She gripped it tight but had to remember not to crack the damn tub.

"All I could think about in that car was that I needed you. That I shouldn't have left the cabin. That you had been right," Liana murmured.

She slid her hands down Eddie's breasts. She took her time bathing them and ensuring they were clean. Eddie's nipples were hard as diamonds. Her breath stalled as Liana played with them.

Her eyes flicked upward to meet Eddie's. "I knew that I didn't want to die. I wanted to see you again."

Her hand dipped beneath the water's surface. Eddie's heart raced at the thought of the fear that had consumed Liana. She blinked and had to force her bear down. The animal paced inside her, begging to be let out.

Our mate is taking care of us, she hissed to it.

The bear paused, and Eddie felt her slight confusion. This wasn't something they had ever considered.

"I would have never allowed that wolf to touch you," Eddie bit out through clenched teeth. Her fangs descended through her gums. It took everything she had to keep from leaning forward to mark Liana as hers. She may have called herself Eddie's mate, but Eddie needed to make sure Liana understood what that truly meant. Especially since Eddie was an alpha.

"I know that. When I saw a bear arrive, I knew it was you without a doubt," Liana whispered.

She leaned forward and brushed her lips over Eddie's. The move allowed her breasts to press against Eddie's. A growl vibrated from Eddie's chest. She took hold of Liana's face and brought it back to hers. She captured Liana's mouth in a hard kiss that allowed her to show how much she needed her. It was possessive and hot.

Eddie held her tight and plundered her mouth. Liana's arms wrapped around her neck as she held on. She was not shy in returning the kiss. The water in the tub sloshed around. They both ignored the water that flew out and landed on the floor.

"You are mine. To protect. To cherish. To love." Eddie tore her lips away from Liana's. She trailed hot kisses along Liana's chin and jawline. She nuzzled her neck and smoothed her hands down to cup Liana's firm bottom.

"Love?" Liana gasped.

Eddie would explain later how it worked for shifters. Love was instant the moment a shifter found their mate. It was fate. She just hoped that one day Liana would come to love her.

Eddie captured her lips again in another sizzling kiss. Liana moaned into the kiss, her hips grinding down on Eddie's lap. As much she wanted to take her out of the tub at that moment, she knew they needed to finish bathing first.

They quickly washed all of the grime, dirt, and blood off them. Eddie stood and lifted Liana out of the water. She stepped out of the tub and snagged their towels. They dried off and wrapped the towels around them. Eddie was no longer able to wait. She lifted Liana in her arms and carried her out of the bathroom.

Chapter Ten

Eddie didn't listen to her complain that she could walk. The woman stalked out of the bathroom carrying her as if she were afraid she'd disappear. She wrapped her arm around Eddie's neck and held on. Hearing Eddie say that she was her mate sent a warm feeling through her.

Maybe it was being trapped in the cabin with Eddie for the past couple of days, but she had already known she'd developed feelings for the bear shifter. There was not going to be another for her.

The living room was once again warm. Eddie gently sat her down on the couch while she took the blankets and arranged them in their sleeping palette. Once she was satisfied the bedding was to her standards, Eddie motioned for her. Liana stood and unwrapped the towel from around her body. She allowed it to fall to the floor. Eddie's amber gaze locked in on her as she walked toward her.

Liana stopped in front of her. Eddie turned and sat on the floor.

"This needs to go," Liana murmured.

She untucked Eddie's towel and pushed it off her. Eddie's body was magnificent to behold. Her muscular frame, her soft breasts, and her long legs drew Liana to her. Those long legs needed to spread open for her.

Liana wanted to please her.

She knelt before her and wrapped her arms around Eddie's neck. She kissed Eddie as if her life depended on it. Eddie allowed her to control the kiss this time. Liana's tongue swept inside Eddie's mouth. She tasted of power and honey. It was a combination that described Eddie.

Eddie's arms wrapped around her waist and held Liana to her. Liana broke the kiss and left hot, open-mouth kisses along Eddie's skin. She was still warm and smelled of the soap they had used to wash themselves. It was a sweet and sultry scent.

Liana boldly pushed Eddie down. She tried to grab Liana's arms, but she shoved her hands away.

"Let me," Liana murmured.

Eddie rested on her elbows and watched her. Liana moved down and captured one of her nipples in her mouth. She held Eddie's gaze and suckled. She rolled the bud with her tongue while reaching up to grip the other mound. A low growl shook Eddie's chest, but she didn't say a word. There was something resting in her eyes that Liana couldn't read. She blinked and focused on the perfect breast she held. She switched and brought the other one to her mouth. She bathed the entire mound with her tongue, sliding the nipple in between her lips.

Liana allowed her free hand to trail down Eddie's torso. The ridged lines of her muscles needed to be tasted. She released the nipple and moved farther down Eddie's body. Eddie fell back onto the bedding and spread her legs so Liana could settle between them.

She traced each abdominal ridge with her tongue. The woman's body was a masterpiece and deserved to be worshipped as she had done to Liana's body. When she arrived at Eddie's core, she inhaled sharply and brought in the scent of her woman. Eddie's mons had a small strip of hair, but the rest was bare. Liana's core clenched at the sight of her slick pussy. She pressed soft kisses to Eddie's inner thighs then reached up and spread open her labia to reveal her pink pearl.

The slickness that coated her channel called to Liana. She couldn't help but bend her head down so she could taste Eddie's honey. She slid her tongue along the slit and gathered all of the juices that ran out of Eddie. A groan escaped her at the taste that exploded on her tongue.

She couldn't help but devour Eddie. She couldn't get enough of this woman, and the way she'd drawn orgasms from Liana, she wanted to make sure she returned the favor. Eddie moaned, and the sound sent a wave of desire to Liana's core. She continued to focus on Eddie's clit while she pushed two fingers deep inside her.

"Liana," Eddie moaned.

Her hips rose to meet Liana's hand. She gave her slow, teasing strokes while not abandoning her swollen clit. Liana felt empowered that this large alpha woman was trembling underneath her touch. Liana wanted Eddie to feel as desired as she felt when she looked at her. Creamy liquid slipped out of her and covered Liana's fingers. She bit back a smile at the amount of Eddie's honey. Her moans grew louder, her hips undulating from the bedding. Liana shook her head and hummed, increasing the rhythm of her fingers sinking into Eddie.

It didn't take much longer for Eddie to be writhing on the pallet and calling her name. Liana twisted her fingers around and slammed them harder into Eddie. Her hands gripped the blankets, and her hips lifted from the bed. Her muscles grew taut. A roar fell from Eddie's lips as she reached her peak.

Eddie's body trembled, but Liana didn't stop. She pushed her fingers deep within Eddie's channel that clutched her tight while she continued to suckle on her clit. Eddie's fingers fisted her hair and held on while she rode Liana's tongue.

Liana glanced up and took in the magnificent sight of her strong woman basking in the aftermath of her orgasm. Her hips slowed until they finally paused. Liana released her swollen button. She withdrew her fingers and cleaned them off before she turned back to Eddie's center. Her legs were still wide open, presenting her slick pussy. Liana took her time cleaning all of her release from her.

Once she was done, she slowly crawled up over Eddie and rested her hands on either side of her head. Eddie's eyes flew open. There was something in her eyes that was different. The amber was bright, and a growl ripped from her. She flipped them over before Liana could even blink. Her fangs peeked underneath her top lip.

"Liana," Eddie whispered.

She leaned down and nuzzled Liana's shoulder. Her tongue bathed Liana's skin. She inhaled, and Liana slid her arms around Eddie's waist to hold her close. She closed her eyes and felt it in her gut what Eddie's bear needed.

"Do it," Liana moaned. She wasn't a shifter, but she knew what Eddie wanted. If she was Eddie's mate, then she would want to claim her properly. It was a big step, and at this moment, Liana yearned for it. She craved the mark.

She had to belong to Eddie.

"You don't know what you are asking." Eddie lifted her head.

There was a longing in her eyes, and it was

then that Liana knew she'd been right. Eddie was desperate to put her mark on her.

You are mine. To protect. To cherish. To love.

Eddie's words echoed in her mind. Liana may be human, but she believed in fate, too, and if that was how she ended up stranded in a winter snowstorm with Eddie, then it was meant to be.

She was meant to be right here with Eddie.

And she was meant to be claimed.

Liana tilted her head to the side to present her full neck and shoulder to Eddie. She was never more sure of something in her life.

"Make me yours," she whispered. She reached up and cupped the back of Eddie's head and brought it back to the crook of her neck. "Make this official."

A growl rumbled deep within Eddie. She dragged her wide tongue along Liana's shoulder. A piercing pain engulfed Liana. She bit back a cry at the intensity. Eddie's fangs sank deep into her muscle. The pain took over her, but her core clenched. Eddie slipped her fingers between her legs and stroked her clit. The pleasure replaced the pain, and soon she was climaxing on Eddie's fingers. Eddie lifted her head and licked the wound, but Liana was too busy trembling and shaking from the force of her orgasm that rushed in and took her breath away.

She lay back and blinked. She had never had an almost immediate orgasm like that before. Her breaths were coming in pants, and her body jerked from the remnants of the climax. Eddie brought her fingers up to her mouth, but Liana took hold of her wrist and brought her fingers to her lips. She licked off her own juices from Eddie's fingers.

Eddie growled softly and watched Liana clean her fingers.

"Mate," Eddie rasped. She gripped Liana's chin in her hands, while a small smile played on her lips.

"Yes, I'm your mate," Liana whispered. Her shoulder ached from the proof. She would wear the mark proudly.

"As I am yours," Eddie said. She kissed Liana with a tenderness that brought tears to her eyes. She dropped her gaze down to Liana's shoulder. "I'll have to take care of this wound, too. Once it heals, you will be marked as mine forever."

"Good," Liana replied.

She brought Eddie's face down to hers and

captured her lips with hers. Their kiss deepened. Their legs became entangled with each other as they continued. Liana sighed and opened her legs so Eddie could settle between them.

The storm may be raging outside, but she was safe with the woman who had just put her claim on her. There was nowhere else she'd rather be than in Eddie's arms.

Chapter Eleven

The storm finally broke. It had been three days since that last wave of the storm had dumped what seemed to be an endless amount of snow.

For a long moment, Liana stood at the large window in the living room. She blinked at the brightness that streamed in through the frosted glass. Sunlight glittered over acres of snow-laden trees and blanketed hills. The world had been transformed from raging white chaos to a soft, quiet stillness. The sky was a bright crystal blue she hadn't seen since she'd left the airport and crashed the car into a ditch and was rescued by her fated mate.

A love that had found her in the middle of a storm.

If that wasn't fate, she didn't know what was.

Behind her, Eddie moved through the cabin with her natural grace that made Liana's heart warm with love. These few days together and the sight of Eddie, barefoot, hair damp from her shower, wrapped up in a long-sleeved sweater and jeans, made her stomach flutter like a schoolgirl with her first crush.

Except this wasn't anything as innocent as that. The past few days, the claiming had been just that. Eddie had barely allowed her out of their bed. Her body tingled in all of the perfect places. She bit her lip and thought of the intimate moments they had shared. Her throat still felt a little scratchy from all of the screaming Eddie had her doing.

Her shoulder was still slightly sore where Eddie had placed her mark. Her core clenched at the memory of Eddie's fangs sinking into her. The mark, almost healed, would forever show that she had been claimed by her alpha bear.

"The truck is dug out and ready," Eddie announced. She came to stand alongside Liana. Her amber-eyed gaze swept the yard before coming to settle on Liana. It flicked to Liana's shoulder before meeting her eyes. She smelled of cedar soap and a hint of honey. "Road will probably be a little rough, but I'm sure we'll make it fine."

"Well, if we slide into a ditch, I know of a bear who has a nearby cabin we'll be safe at," Liana teased.

That earned her a chuckle from Eddie. She wrapped an arm around Liana and brought her close. Liana leaned into her, loving the feeling of their bodies pressed against each other.

"Time to go?"

"Yes." Eddie hesitated for a moment. She studied Liana as if she was waiting for her to change her mind about something. "It's time for us to go home."

"Our home?" Liana asked.

That earned her a growl from her bear. Eddie's chest vibrated from the sound.

"Yes, our home," Eddie murmured. She leaned down and dropped a soft kiss to Liana's lips. She lifted her head and smiled. "We need to go or else these clothes will be off and it'll be another three days before we leave."

"Don't tease me with a good time." Liana laughed.

Eddie's eyes darkened as her hands slipped

down to cup Liana's bottom. She backed away from her mate and shook her head. Unfortunately, they couldn't stay here hidden away together forever. They had to return to reality.

"We'll have plenty of time for that later. After you take me home."

The last three days had been magical. The storm had trapped them, but it had also gifted them time. They'd been wrapped up in blankets, learned about each other in the dim glow of the fire, spent plenty of time touching and exploring each other. Eddie wasn't always a soft woman, her alpha bear instincts were sharp, sometimes overwhelming, but Liana would have to blame herself. She had a certainly tested the bear, but Eddie was always gentle when it came to her. Even when she was upset with her.

Liana thought of all the moments she'd come to love. Eddie brushing snow from her face when they'd gone outside to get fresh air; Liana noting Eddie's focused alpha look she had when she studied something. These days in the cabin had allowed them to truly get to know one another. Liana would always be grateful for the storm and what it had gifted her.

It had given her a new life. But now that it

was over, it was time for them to go back to reality. The world would be waiting on them.

They finished packing the little items they were taking with them. Liana had her belongings from the car. She would call the rental company later to report the accident. She reached for her coat that had finally dried out and zipped it up. She walked across the room where her boots were sitting by the couch. She sat and slid the first one on. She had to admit that her ankle felt a hundred times better. She'd barely felt any pain. She wiggled it around. Eddie had insisted on wrapping it again.

She glanced up and found Eddie standing near the doorway silently watching her.

"You don't need to hover over me." Liana chuckled. She slipped the other boot on and bent over to tie them up.

"I'm not hovering," Eddie replied.

"You are. You have checked on my ankle at least twice since you wrapped it. I'm fine." Liana smiled and held her leg up in the air as if to show off the healed sprain.

"I am just making sure my mate is healing."

"And I appreciate it. I do." Liana stood, and again, no pain.

Eddie gave her nod and came into the room and grabbed her bag that was resting on the floor. The cabin had been cleaned from top to bottom. They'd put everything back where it belonged. The hearth was now no longer burning a bright flame. Only a few embers remained with a slight glow.

Liana glanced around at what had been their haven and sighed. She would miss this place. As if sensing her thoughts, Eddie took her hand and brought it to her lips.

"We'll come back. Let's get you home." She kissed the back of it.

Liana gave a nod and snagged her belongings then followed Eddie out of the cabin. She headed over to the waiting truck while Eddie locked the door. Once they were in, the engine roared to life. Eddie guided the vehicle down the long winding drive. Liana eyed the cabin in the side mirror and watched it get smaller as they drove off.

They arrived at the narrow mountain road. It was still half-buried in places, the edges drifted with snow so deep it looked like untouched cloud banks. Ice shimmered in patches, and every few turns the truck fishtailed just enough to send Liana's pulse racing.

Eddie drove with a confidence that Liana admired. The road finally evened out, and Liana relaxed slightly. She settled in her seat and watched the scenery blur past in the bright, cold winter colors.

Her phone buzzed faintly in the cup holder. It was the first time she'd heard it make a noise in days. She snatched it up and stared at the screen. There were multiple missed calls from so many of her family and friends.

She had bars for a signal!

"Oh, goodness," she breathed. "My sister. She probably thinks I'm dead in a ditch somewhere."

"Call her." Eddie shot her an empathetic glance before turning back to the road.

Liana tapped on her sister's last missed call. The phone rang once before it was answered by hysterically crying and shouting.

"Liana? Is that you? Oh God, Liana. Where the hell have you been? Do you know what—I thought—you can't just...why haven't you called?"

Liana squeezed her eyes shut, feeling the

prickling of tears. She inhaled sharply at the pain in her sister's voice.

"I promise I'm okay," she said softly. She wished she would have been able to call her sister. Had the shoe been on the other foot, she would have been a mess, too. She repeated herself at the sobbing that filled her ear. "I'm okay."

"You just disappeared! Terri and I had the police looking for you, but they said this storm was one of the worst they'd seen in a while. Liana, I thought we'd lost you."

The words broke something in Liana. The tears flowed down her cheeks.

"I'm sorry." Liana whispered. "My car crashed. I got stuck out there in the storm. But I...I found shelter. Someone rescued and helped me."

"Someone?" Jorrie sniffed. "What do you mean, someone?"

She glanced at Eddie who reached over and gave her thigh a squeeze. Liana reached up and brushed the wetness from her cheeks.

"I met someone," Liana shared. A small smile played on her lips. "Someone I care about...a lot."

"Liana English! Don't you tell me you disappeared in the middle of the worst storm in history and come out with a new girlfriend!"

Eddie snorted. She could obviously hear her sister's side of the conversation. Liana's cheeks warmed.

"I'll explain everything, okay? I just need to call Terri next," Liana said.

"Oh, no! You are not hanging up without giving me all the details!"

"I promise I will call you back once we are settled at her place," Liana said.

"Her place?" Jorrie shrieked. "We are so talking about this. You better call me back or I am hopping on the next plane out of here to Montana!"

"I promise," Liana whispered. "I love you, sis."

"You better! I thought we'd have to start planning your funeral."

They disconnected the call with Liana pinky swearing she'd call her sister back. She then placed a call to Terri and had almost the exact same conversation. After the second call, Liana figured she'd wait before she called everyone else back. She wiped the tears from her cheeks. She hated that her family had suffered while she had been tucked away in the snowy mountains.

Eddie reached across and entwined their fingers together.

"It will be our place," Eddie reminded her.

Liana's heart stuttered. She gave Eddie's hand a squeeze. Love filled her chest at the warmth that radiated from Eddie. Was it too soon to tell Eddie she loved her? They hadn't known each other long, but Liana was sure what she felt was love. The mark on her was definitely proof that Eddie wanted her.

But as a shifter, did that mean love?

"Yes, our place," she murmured. She'd figure out everything later. Right now, this felt right, and she wasn't going to miss out on this opportunity with Eddie.

They continued down the mountain road with sunlight glittering across the snow. After all of the chaos it had caused, now it was a peaceful white blanket that surrounded them. It reminded Liana of a new start.

Something she had gained with Eddie. A new life. She looked forward to embarking on her new journey with her mate.

Chapter Twelve

The ride down the mountain took much longer than Eddie would have liked. Every twist and patch of black ice kept her laser focused. She had to keep her mate safe. Her bear prowled beneath her skin the entire time. She, too, was anxious to get Liana home. She was restless and watchful yet still angry about the feral wolf who had hunted her down. She hadn't caught wind of the wolf ever since that night. Even with Liana next to her in the vehicle, warm and enticing, Eddie couldn't shake the primal urgency that hummed within her.

Protect. Provide. Cherish.

All of those qualities ran through her veins now at the thought of the claiming mark they had put on Liana. Her mark would forever be a symbolism of Eddie's claim on Liana. Everyone would know that Liana belonged to Eddie.

When the town came into view, small and quiet under the melting snow, something eased inside her.

This was her town. Her territory. Liana would be safe here.

Liana's fingers were laced with hers. Liana's thumb brushed along Eddie's knuckles unconsciously as she stared out the window at the scenery. Eddie's chest swelled at the thought that she had her mate with her.

They turned down the long gravel road that would lead to her—their—home. A wide house with a wraparound porch sat tucked near towering pines. It was magnificent place that she'd had built a few years ago. When she had built it, she'd had always imagined a mate to share it with her.

Now that was today.

Eddie's breath seized. Awe filled her that Liana would be sharing this home with her. Sleeping in her bed, cooking in the kitchen, and lounging on the couch. The image that came to her mind filled her with immense pleasure.

Her bear rumbled her approval.

But the moment they got closer to the house, she saw them.

A small greeting party. Selen, Nick, and Abe.

Three broad-shouldered silhouettes against the snow. They were waiting for her. Her beta and two of the enforcers.

"Of course they are here." Eddie blew out a deep breath.

"Do you normally have a welcoming crew to greet you when you come home?" Liana asked. She tilted her head and studied them.

"My clan can be as protective of me as I am of them." Eddie chuckled. She guided the truck up to the house and parked in front of the garage.

"Should I be nervous?" Liana asked.

"Never," Eddie replied immediately. She would never have to worry. The three bears waiting on them would protect Liana with their lives if need be. As the mate of the alpha, Liana would always feel safe. "You are my mate. An extension of me. You'll be respected here."

"Even though I'm not a bear?"

"It doesn't matter." Eddie reached up and caressed her cheek.

Her bears were patiently waiting for them to get out of the truck. The moment she killed the engine, Selen made her way to them with Nick and Abe behind her.

Eddie opened the door and stepped out of the vehicle. Immediately, the three of them dipped their heads in submission. The shift in the air was automatic. A ripple of dominance Eddie didn't consciously summon. Her bear rose in her chest, proud and fierce that they defended this territory and would now get to introduce their mate to some of her closest people.

Selen straightened and stood with her hair behind her back. The beta had been by Eddie's side since she'd taken over their clan. There was a curiosity in her gaze, but she held back.

"Welcome home, Alpha," Selen said. "I trust your vacation was restful."

"In a way." Eddie smirked. She would have to put Selen out of her misery soon and share her adventures on the mountain.

And it was certainly an adventure.

Nick and Abe offered their greetings as well. Their gazes drifted to the truck and landed on Liana. Eddie reined in her bear who wanted to roar to warn them off their woman, but she knew she wouldn't need to. Soon they would sense that Liana was claimed.

Eddie moved around the truck to open Liana's door herself. The second Liana stepped out, her scent lifted in the cold air, and Eddie's bear pressed hard on her chest. Her beast wanted to be let out. She was territorial, possessive, ready to defend her against the world.

All eyes were on Liana. Eddie led her around the vehicle.

"Everyone," Eddie began. Pride swelled hard in her chest as she brought Liana to her side. "This is Liana English. My mate. Liana, this is my beta, Selen, and two of my finest enforcers, Nick and Abe."

Gasps went around. Selen broke out in a wide smile and gave an accepting nod to Liana. Selen, who had recently mated, had been through hell and high water when it came to her partner. She'd faced an alpha bear from another clan in order to claim Rose. It had been an arrangement to join two clans to share resources. Selen had handled everything, and now she was a happily mated woman.

"Congratulations and welcome, Liana. My mate, Rose, will be thrilled to know that the alpha has finally found her mate," Selen said. She folded her arms across her chest.

Rose was a wonderful member of their clan. Her local apothecary shop had been a welcomed addition to their town.

"Welcome, Liana," Nick said.

"Yes, welcome. I'm sure you will love it here." Abe offered a smile to Liana.

Eddie pushed down a growl from her bear. Her animal didn't like the fact that two unmated bears were so close to her female. Nick and Abe were two of her most loyal bears. They would never betray her. They even kept a respectable distance from Liana. A newly mated bear was a dangerous one.

"It's so nice to meet you all." Liana gave them a small wave. She slipped her arm around Eddie's waist and leaned into her.

Eddie dropped an arm around Liana's shoulders to hold her close. It pleased her to have Liana showing a little possessiveness of her own, even if she didn't realize she did it.

"Terri called me this morning. She said her friend who she had reported missing had finally contacted her." Selen gave a nod in Liana's direction. "She had called earlier this week when you hadn't shown. She was worried sick about you. We attempted to search, but in this storm, it was too dangerous."

"Thank you. I really appreciate it. That was a nasty storm, but luckily enough, someone found me and kept me safe." Liana turned her eyes to Eddie with a wide grin. "I have to call her and my sister back. I pinky swore with both of them."

"You can once you're settled," Eddie said firmly. She gave Liana's shoulder a squeeze before she turned back to Selen. She wanted Liana to herself a little while longer before the entire clan met her. "I'm sure you have updates for me. Let's meet later tonight after I get Liana comfortable."

"Yes, of course. There's not much to share, but we do need to discuss a few things. All of it can wait." Selen motioned for the enforcers to follow her to the oversized SUV that awaited them.

They waited until Selen and the enforcers were driving down the gravel road before Eddie turned to Liana.

"Come, mate. Let me take you inside," she said.

They walked up the stairs to the porch and stopped on the top step. Liana was silent and had an unreadable expression.

"Are you okay?" Eddie asked.

"That was interesting," she said. Her eyes widened as if she realized what she'd said. "In a good way. I knew you were the alpha of your clan, but seeing them waiting for us just made it seem all the more real."

Eddie cupped her face in her hands. Her thumbs caressed Liana's soft skin. She offered a smile to Liana before she pressed a kiss to her lips.

"You just don't know what you are in for. When my entire clan finds out I'm mated, there will be tons of people who are going to want to meet you and get to know you, but have no worries. They will all be kind, respectful, but most of all—excited."

"Excited?" Liana laughed.

"Yes, they were practically demanding that I get mated. When I returned from my little vacation, I was going to reach out to other clans and do what Selen did," she admitted. She would have settled for a mating of convenience for the good of her clan.

But now she wouldn't have to. Fate had delivered her mate to her.

She led Liana toward the front door. The porch creaked underneath their feet. The house smelled like cedar, warm wood, and the faint remnants of safe incense she'd burned before she'd left for her mountain retreat. When Eddie opened the door and Liana stepped inside, it suddenly felt more like home than it had ever had before.

Liana took everything in. The vaulted ceiling, the stone fireplace, the worn leather couch that Eddie loved so much.

"This is nice," Liana gasped. She walked into the living room and turned around.

Seeing her in the home did something to Eddie.

"Anything you want to change, we can," Eddie said. She wanted to ensure that Liana felt that this was her home, too.

"Change? Why would I change anything?" Liana spun around and stared at Eddie.

She walked across the room and stood in front of Liana. Her eyes were wide.

"I want to make sure this feels like your home, too." She reached out and cupped Liana's cheek. She lowered her forehead to hers. "You are my mate. My partner. My heart. I want you to feel comfortable. Put your stamp on our home."

Liana blinked. Her breath caught as she studied Eddie. Her throat moved, but no words came out.

But three certain words rose from Eddie. She didn't hold back. She wanted to make sure that Liana knew exactly what she felt for her.

"I love you, Liana."

Silence settled around them. Liana's breath shuddered out of her, and tears filled her eyes.

"Eddie…"

But Eddie wasn't going to stop with your just those words.

"I've loved you from the moment I first pulled you from that car. When you screamed for me after falling into the creek. When you tried to talk me into letting you go with me to get your things from the car. The point I'm making is that I have been falling for you since the moment I sensed there was someone in trouble who needed my help."

That was the honest truth. Her bear had

known. Fate had known she'd deposited Eddie's mate for her to find.

A tear slid down Liana's cheek. Eddie gently brushed it away. She hadn't meant to make her cry. She bit her lip, for once unsure of what to expect. She was an alpha, a bear who was in control of an entire clan. A woman who was strong, determined, fierce, and had fought to preserve her position in her clan, and now, here she was, unsure if the woman in front of her loved her.

"I love you, too," Liana whispered. Her voice trembled. "I love you so much it scares me. Here I was, thinking that all of this happened so fast—"

"Because it was mean to be," Eddie interrupted. "There is no need for you to fear anything when it comes to me and you."

Liana melted into her. She slid her hands up Eddie's back and gripped her tight. They stood there for a long moment. Eddie leaned back slightly so she could look at her.

"The clan will want to meet you soon. As much as I want to delay it, I won't be able to. Once word it out that you are here, we will need to hold a meet and greet. I'm sure the council will arrange it."

"I can handle it. Especially if it is your clan," Liana said.

"Our clan," Eddie corrected her. She wore Eddie's claiming mark, and that signified she was a member of the clan as well. Eddie pressed a kiss to Liana's forehead. "Are you sure you don't mind moving your life here? This will be a big change from Denver."

"This is where you are and where I need to be."

The words wrapped around Eddie like a warm hug. She scooped Liana into her arms and carried her deeper into the house.

"Welcome home, my love," Eddie whispered.

Liana's arms draped around her neck as she held on. From the moment she'd met Liana, she'd wanted to do this.

"I'm going to assume we are about to consummate our mating in our home?" Liana whispered. She nuzzled Eddie's neck while sprinkling hot little kisses along it.

Eddie inhaled and sped up her pace. Her mate somehow always knew what she was thinking.

Epilogue

The community center buzzed with celebration. Laughter, clinking glasses, upbeat music, and the hum of the townsfolk of Lurton gathered for a night they would be sure to remember. Everywhere Liana turned, someone was smiling at her or reaching out to clasp her hands or pull Eddie in for a hug.

She had never been the center of attention before like this. Weddings she'd attend had all been small, intimate affairs. Family celebrations were cozy dinners. But this was a full-on clan celebration for the mating of their alpha.

Eddie and her.

And the entire town had to be there. If she hadn't already been in love with Eddie, she certainly would have fallen in love with her tonight. The devotion to Eddie was breathtakingly beautiful. Everyone loved their alpha.

Compliment after compliment washed over her. Each one filled her chest with an overwhelming sense of belonging.

Eddie stood tall and proud with her and firmly clasped her hand around Liana's. Her thumb stroked slow circles against Liana's skin. Every time Eddie looked at her, her amber eyes softened. Her bear appeared to be content. She didn't growl as much as she used to.

Selen approached wearing a dark sweater and jeans, while her mate, Rose, was in a deep-green dress.

"It's a beautiful celebration," Rose said.

She reached out and squeezed Liana's hand. Her eyes were bright and welcoming. They had met several times since Liana had arrived in Lurton. It had only taken the council a week to organize their mating celebration.

"I'm so happy for the two of you," Rose added.

"Thank you." Liana gave her hand a squeeze before letting it go.

"May your union be blessed, Eddie." Selen

snagged her own mate and brought her close to her.

"Fate chose us and threw us together. I'm just glad I was able to find her in time," Eddie said.

"I'm glad, too. I sure as hell didn't want to freeze to death," Liana muttered.

They all shared a laugh together. Before Liana could say anything else, a familiar voice hollered her name. She turned just in time to see her sister barreling right toward her.

"Jorrie!"

The two fell into a hug mixed with crying and laughter. Jorrie pulled back and studied her.

"If you ever scare me like that again. I don't even know what I would do with you," Jorrie said.

It felt so good to see her. Liana almost didn't want to let her go.

"I'm sorry. I truly am, but I seriously didn't have a way to call you. That mountain had no service," Liana explained for the hundredth time. But she didn't care. Her sister was here in Lurton. Liana felt a presence at her back. She spun on her heels and found Eddie standing behind her. "Sis, let me introduce you to my mate, Eddie."

"Hello. Welcome to Lurton, Jorrie," Eddie said, taking Jorrie's hand in hers in a quick shake.

"Oh my God. Eddie? Really? You didn't tell me she was built like a goddess-warrior-lumberjack." Jorrie gestured wildly.

Liana snorted hard and fell into a fit of laughter at her correct depiction of Eddie. Now that Jorrie had said it, she couldn't unsee it.

"That's a compliment?" Eddie arched an eyebrow.

"It is." Terri blew in and joined them. She wrapped Liana up in her arms for a strong hug.

Since she'd decided to stay in Lurton, she'd already jumped in to help with Terri and the baby. Terri signaled between Liana and Jorrie. She grinned and shook her head.

"It'll take a minute to understand these two. Just give it a little time, Alpha."

Liana grinned and stepped back. She felt so damn happy that her sister was here along with her best friend. Tonight was an amazing night, and she was enjoying herself.

Jorrie nudged Liana. "And she's hot, too!"

"Jorrie!" Liana's eyes went wide as she stared at Jorrie who just shrugged.

Eddie's low, amused growl rumbled in her

chest which prompted a few of the clan members to glance over with fond smiles. Terri steered Jorrie away with the offer to introduce her around.

Well-wishers continued to stop by from Eddie's family, friends, and community elders. They couldn't take five steps without someone getting their attention, all of them desiring to embrace the newly mated couple. Liana felt welcomed by everyone. Eddie had been right. They treated her as if she were an extension of Eddie. Liana found herself smiling, laughing, and hugging strangers who accepted her because she belonged to Eddie.

This was her new community.

"Want to sneak out of here?" Eddie murmured in her ear.

"I thought you would never ask." Liana grinned. She didn't mind meeting everyone, but literally the entire town had showed up tonight, and this was a bit overwhelming.

Eddie took her by her hand and guided her through the crowd. They grabbed their coats from the closet room and eased out the back door unnoticed by most.

The night air was crisp and stung Liana's

cheeks. She breathed in deeply and allowed the cool air to calm her nerves. Snow blanketed the edges of the clearing of the parking lot. It gleamed brightly under the full moon.

They walked hand in hand toward Eddie's truck. Liana remained close to her side. She didn't want to put much distance between them while riding high on the love they had received from the clan members.

Moonlight softened the strong angles of Eddie's face. She looked peaceful and content. She was so breathtakingly beautiful that Liana's heart skipped a beat. They had parked at the back of the lot. The walk wasn't long, but it allowed them to get some fresh air.

When they reached the truck, Eddie gave Liana's hand a gentle tug, turning her to face her fully. For a moment, neither of them spoke. Eddie lifted her hand and brushed her thumb across Liana's cheek. Liana leaned into her touch. Her eyes fluttered closed as she savored the warmth from Eddie's palm.

When she opened her eyes again, Eddie's expression was tender in a way she saved only for Liana.

"My mate," Eddie whispered. She leaned down and kissed Liana.

It was slow and deep. It was a vow and a promise of love wrapped together. Liana fisted the front of Eddie's coat and pulled her close. She melted into her warmth, her strength, and her everything.

When they finally parted, Eddie rested her forehead on Liana's.

"My forever," Eddie murmured.

Tears blurred her vision. Liana sniffed and gave a small nod.

"Forever," she echoed.

"Under the full moon, I am making a promise to love you, cherish you, and protect you as long as there is breath in my lungs."

Tears slipped down Liana's cheeks. She smiled at Eddie and pressed against her.

"I promise to love you, protect you, and cherish you as well," Liana said.

Eddie kissed her again, this time brief and hard. It took Liana's breath away.

Faint sounds from the celebration drifted through the cold night air. With the moon beaming down bearing a witness to their promises, Liana knew that fate hadn't just saved her that night.

It had brought the love of her life to her.

ABOUT THE AUTHOR

Ariel Marie is an author who loves the paranormal, action and hot steamy romance. She combines all three in each and every one of her stories. For as long as she can remember, she has loved vampires, shifters and every creature you can think of. This even rolls over into her favorite movies. She loves a good action packed thriller! Throw a touch of the supernatural world in it and she's hooked!

Sign up for Ariel Marie's newsletter!
Scan the QR Code to get all the latest news from Ariel Marie!

For more information visit:
www.thearielmarie.com

The Nightstar Shifters

No wolf can resist the call to mate.

Strong female wolves are in search of their mate. The desire is strong for these women who long to find the one person meant for them.

They are fierce and determined, putting their trust in fate.

If you love lesbian wolf shifter romance filled with action and adventure, then you will love the Nightstar Shifters series.

Ready to start the Nightstar Shifters? Click HERE to download book one!

The Immortal Reign Series

Vampires and Humans. Are they meant to be together? One drop of blood will control their futures.

After the war between vampires and humankind, Earth was never the same. This new world was dangerous, and vampires were on the hunt for their fated mates. The installation of the draft should have made things simpler, but all it did was create chaos.

Humans didn't want to conform to the new ways of life.

Vampires had no problems making them.

Enter this new dark and sexy world full of lesbian vampire romance. The Immortal Reign series is an adult-themed paranormal romance that you will want to sink your teeth into. If you love action-packed, sizzling hot wlw romances, then this is the series for you.

Start the Immortal Reign series today! Grab book one today!

ALSO BY ARIEL MARIE

Taming Her Mate

Teague

Adrian

Nicu